KHALED

KHALED

F. MARION CRAWFORD

INTRODUCTION BY LEE WEINSTEIN

Wildside Press

New Jersey • California • Ohio • New York

Published by:

Wildside Press
P.O. Box 45
Gillette, NJ 07933
www.wildsidepress.com

First Wildside Press edition: April, 2001

KHALED

INTRODUCTION

In 1909, F. Marion Crawford was one of the most widely read novelists of the English-speaking world. His fame was such that when he became seriously ill in March of that year, his progress was reported on the front page of *The New York Times* on a daily basis for the last week of his life. His obituary spilled over onto page 2 of the *Times*. In the Italian village where he lived, all the shops were immediately closed upon his death, the door of each bearing a sign saying "closed for public mourning."

He had written over 40 novels by the time of his death, as well as a play and several histories of Italy.

Today, like Robert W. Chambers, Edward Lucas White, and Edward Bulwer-Lytton, he is little remembered for the bulk of his work, which like theirs consisted largely of romances and historical fiction. The works of these writers that have survived the test of time are for the most part fantasies and tales of horror. Today, Crawford is remembered to some extent for a few fantasy novels and primarily for the ghostly tales in this collection.

Francis Marion Crawford was born in Bagni di Lucca in Italy in 1854, of American parents. He was the youngest of four children and the only boy. His family was an artistic one. His father was the noted sculptor Thomas Crawford, most famous for his "Armed Liberty" atop the Capitol Building in Washington, D.C. and for the monument to George Washington in Richmond, Virginia. His mother was Louisa Ward, a sister of Julia Ward Howe (who wrote the "Battle Hymn of the Republic") and Samuel Ward (who had also done some writing). His sister Mary wrote under her married name of Mrs. Hugh Fraser, and became well known at the time for her novels and travel books. His biography was written by his cousin,

Maud Howe Elliot, herself the author of a number of biographical and other books.

She describes him, at age 23, as "tall, splendidly built, with a noble head, classic features, and hands and feet of sculpturesque beauty. His eyes were blue, dancing, full of light, real Irish eyes."

Crawford had a colorful and eclectic background and a cosmopolitan education. He was sent at a young age to live in Bordentown, New Jersey, but after the death of his father in 1857 he was returned to Italy at the age of three, where he was taught by a French governess. He attended a school in Concord, New Hampshire between the ages of twelve and fourteen. He went on to study Greek and mathematics in Rome and later studied German, Swedish, and Spanish at Trinity College, Cambridge. He was eventually to master eighteen languages, including Oscan, Tuscan, Hindustani, and Urdu. At the age of 20, he was at Karlsruhe in Baden and then at Heidelberg, where he pursued his studies in languages. At the age of 22 he took up the study of Sanskrit at the University of Rome and became so fascinated by it that he traveled to India. In Bombay, he sold some articles to the *Times of India* and soon became an editor for the *Indian Herald* in Allahabad.

He returned to Rome in 1880 and eventually returned to America to study Sanskrit at Harvard.

His first novel was *Mr. Isaacs* (1882). It was written at the urging of an uncle upon hearing Crawford recount the story of a diamond merchant he had heard about while in India. Although it contains such fantastic elements as astral projection, they are not integral to the plot, and the novel is not a true fantasy. It was upon the instant and sensational success of this book that he decided to become a novelist.

He settled in Italy and spent most of his adult life there. In 1884 he married Elizabeth Berdan, daughter of the American General, Hiram Berdan, inventor of the Berdan rifle. They lived at first in Rome. The following year he bought a villa in Sant' Agnello, Sorrento overlooking the Bay of Naples, which was to remain his home for the rest of his life. They had four children.

Crawford had a reclusive streak, and when the Villa Crawford became a social center, he leased the tower of San Niccola on the coast of Calabria. It was a high forbidding building with thick stone walls perched atop the cliffs overlooking the sea. He retired there when he wanted to write or to seek solitude.

He wrote at least one novel a year, and sometimes two or three, but relatively few of them were fantastic in content.

With the Immortals (1888), concerns an inventor who resurrects the spirits of famous men. Its focus is not horror, but consists largely of conversations between the inventor's family and the various ghosts. Some critics feel it is not so much a novel as platform Crawford employed to expound his ideas.

The Witch of Prague (1891), his only novel length horror story, is about a young woman whose powers of witchcraft stem from her mastery of hypnotism.

Khaled (1891), perhaps the most effective of his fantasy novels, is Arabian fantasy sometimes compared to Beckford's *Vathek*. It concerns a genie who is made mortal as a punishment. It was reprinted by Lin Carter as part of the series of adult fantasies he edited for Ballantine Books in the sixties.

His last fantasy novel was *Cecilia, a Story of Modern Rome* (1902). It is a romance in which two lovers are brought together by a series of identical recurring dreams.

In his day, Crawford was the leading advocate of Romanticism in fiction. He set down his philosophy of writing in a book called *The Novel: What It Is* in 1893. In it, he argued that the purpose of the novel is not to instruct but to entertain. In discussing realistic versus romantic fiction, he states his case by saying that "more good can be done by showing men what they may be, ought to be, or can be, than by describing their greatest weaknesses with the highest art."

He considered his writing to be mere entertainment, but he peopled it with vivid characters, often based on real-life counterparts. He set them against meticulously drawn backgrounds of the places he had visited. He was a master at creating atmosphere. And above all, he was a natural born story-teller.

He wrote over 40 novels. But it is his ghostly tales for which he is primarily remembered. These share the vividness of character and setting of his books. Seven of the eight short stories he wrote at various times throughout his career were collected posthumously and published in 1911 under the title *Uncanny Tales* in Europe and *Wandering Ghosts* in the U.S., to generally good reviews.

Toward the end of 1908, an earthquake in southern Italy destroyed Messina and killed over 200,000 people. Crawford spent the last months of his life doing relief work for the refugees. He contracted influenza and developed complications affecting the bronchial tubes and pleura. He died at the age of 54 while still at work on his final novel, a romance.

Today, most of Crawford's work remains out of print. But the Villa Crawford still stands in his home town in Italy and is still known by that name, and entries on him can still be found in most encyclopedias. And his ghostly tales continue to be popular. One can only regret that he did not write more of them.

Lee Weinstein
Philadelphia, 2000

CHAPTER I

KHALED stood in the third heaven, which is the heaven of precious stones, and of Asrael, the angel of Death. In the midst of the light shed by the fruit of the trees Asrael himself is sitting, and will sit until the day of the resurrection from the dead, writing in his book the names of those who are to be born, and blotting out the names of those who have lived their years and must die. Each of the trees has seventy thousand branches, each branch bears seventy thousand fruits, each fruit is composed of seventy thousand diamonds, rubies, emeralds, carbuncles, jacinths, and other precious stones. The stature and proportions of Asrael are so great that his eyes are seventy thousand days' journey apart, the one from the other.

Khaled stood motionless during ten months and thirteen days, waiting until Asrael should rest from his writing and look towards him. Then came the holy night called Al Kadr, the night of peace in which the

B

Koran came down from heaven. Asrael paused, and raising his eyes from the scroll saw Khaled standing before him.

Asrael knew Khaled, who was one of the genii converted to the faith on hearing Mohammed read the Koran by night in the valley Al Nakhlah. He wondered, however, when he saw him standing in his presence; for the genii are not allowed to pass even the gate of the first heaven, in which the stars hang by chains of gold, each star being inhabited by an angel who guards the entrance against the approach of devils.

Asrael looked at Khaled in displeasure, therefore, supposing that he had eluded the heavenly sentinels and concealed an evil purpose. But Khaled inclined himself respectfully.

'There is no Allah but Allah. Mohammed is the prophet of Allah,' he said, thus declaring himself to be of the Moslem genii, who are upright and are true believers.

'How camest thou hither?' asked Asrael.

'By the will of Allah, who sent his angel with me to the gate,' Khaled answered. 'I am come hither that thou mayest write down my name in the book of life and death, that I may be a man on earth, and after an appointed time thou shalt blot it out again and I shall die.'

Asrael gazed at him and knew that this was the will

of Allah, for the angels are thus immediately made
conscious of the divine commands. He took up his pen
to write, but before he had traced the first letter he
paused.

'This is the night Al Kadr,' he said. 'If thou wilt,
tell me therefore thy story, for I am now at leisure to
hear it.'

'Thou knowest that I am of the upright genii,'
Khaled answered, 'and I am well disposed towards
men. In the city of Riad, in Arabia, there rules a
powerful king, the Sultan of the kingdom of Nejed,
blessed in all things save that he has no son to inherit
his vast dominions. One daughter only has been born
to him in his old age, of such marvellous beauty that
even the Black Eyed Virgins enclosed in the fruit of
the tree Sedrat, who wait for the coming of the faithful,
would seem but mortal women beside her. Her eyes
are as the deep water in the wells of Zobeideh when
it is night and the stars are reflected therein. Her hair
is finer than silk, red with henna, and abundant as the
foliage of the young cypress tree. Her face is as fair as
the kernels of young almonds, and her mouth is sweeter
than the mellow date and more fragrant than 'Ood
mingled with ambergris. She possesses moreover all
the virtues which become women, for she is as modest
as she is beautiful and as charitable as she is modest.
From all parts of Arabia and Egypt, and from Syria and

from Persia, and even from Samarkand, from Afghanistan, and from India princes and kings' sons continually come to ask her in marriage, for the fame of her beauty and of her virtues is as wide as the world. But her father, desiring only her happiness, leaves the choice of a husband to herself, and for a long time she refused all her suitors. For there is in the palace at Riad a certain secret chamber from which she can observe all those who come and hear their conversation and see the gifts which they bring with them.

'At last there came as a suitor an unbeliever, a prince of an island by the shores of India, beautiful as the moon, whose speech was honey, and who surpassed all the suitors in riches and in the magnificence of the presents he brought. For he came bearing with him a hundred pounds' weight of pure gold, and five hundred ounces of ambergris, and a great weight of musk and sloes and sandal wood, and rich garments without number, and many woven shawls of Kashmir, of which the least splendid was valued at a thousand sherifs of gold. An innumerable retinue accompanied him, and twenty elephants, and horses without number, besides camels.

'The Sultan's daughter beheld this beautiful prince from her secret hiding-place, and all that he had brought with him. The Sultan received him with kindness and hospitality, but assured him that unless he would re-

nounce idolatry and embrace the true faith he could not
hope to succeed in his purpose. Thereupon he was
much cast down, and soon afterwards, having received
magnificent gifts in his turn, he would have departed
on his way, disappointed and heavy at heart. But
Zehowah sent for her father and entreated him to bid
the young prince remain. "For it is not impossible,"
she said, "that he may yet be converted to the true
faith. And have I the right to refuse to sacrifice my
freedom when the sacrifice may be the means of con-
verting an idolater to the right way? And if I marry
him and go with him to his kingdom, shall we not make
true believers of all his subjects, so that I shall deserve
to be called the mother of the faithful like Ayesha,
beloved by the Prophet, upon whom be peace?" The
Sultan found it hard to oppose this argument which was
founded upon virtue and edified in righteousness. He
therefore entreated the Indian prince to remain and to
profess Islam, promising the hand of Zehowah when he
should be converted.

'Then I heard the prince taking secret counsel with
a certain old man who was with him, who shaved his
face and wore white clothing and ate food which he
prepared for himself alone. The prince told all, and
then the old man counselled him in this way. "Speak
whatsoever words they require of thee," he said, "for
words are but garments wherewith to make the naked-

ness of truth modest and agreeable. And take the woman, and by and by, when we are returned to our own land, if she consent to worship thy gods, it is good; and if not, it is yet good, for thou shalt possess her as thy wife, and her unbelief shall be of consequence only to her own soul, but thy soul shall not be retarded in its progress." And the young prince was pleased, and promised to do as his counsellor advised him.

'So I saw that he was false and that Zehowah's righteousness would be but the means to her sorrow if she were allowed to persist. Therefore in the night, when all were asleep in the palace, I entered into the room where the prince was lying, and I took him in my arms and flew with him to the midst of the Red Desert, and there I slew him and buried him in the sand, for I saw that he was a liar and had determined to be a hypocrite.

'But Allah immediately sent an angel to destroy me because I had put to death a man who was about to become a believer, thereby killing his soul also, since he had not yet made profession of the faith. But I stood up and defended myself, saying that I had slain a hypocrite who had planned in his heart to carry away the daughter of a Moslem. Then the angel asked the truth of the prince's soul, which was sitting upon the red sand that covered the body. The soul answered, weeping, and said: "These are true words, and I am fuel for hell."

"Have I then deserved death?" I asked. "I have killed an unbeliever." The angel answered that I had deserved life; and he would have left me and returned to paradise, but I would not let him go, and I besought him to entreat Allah that I might be allowed to live the life of a mortal man upon earth. "For," I said, "thou sayest that I deserve life. But even if thou destroy me not now I am only one of the genii, who shall all die at the first blast of the trumpet before the resurrection of the dead. Obtain for me therefore that I may have a soul and live a few years, and if I do good I shall then be with the faithful in paradise; and if not, I shall be bound with red-hot chains and burn everlastingly like a sinful man." The angel promised to intercede for me and departed. So I sat down upon the mound of red sand beside the soul of the Indian prince, to wait for the angel's coming again.

'Then the soul reproached me angrily. "But for thee," it said, "I should have married Zehowah and returned to my own people, and although I purposed to be a hypocrite, yet in time Zehowah might have convinced me and I should have believed in my heart. For I now see that there is no Allah but Allah, and that Mohammed is the prophet of Allah. And I should perhaps have died full of years, a good Moslem, and should have entered paradise. Therefore I pray Allah that this may be remembered in thy condemnation." At

these words I was very angry and reviled the soul,
scoffing at it. "No doubt Allah will hear thy prayer,"
I answered, "and will hear also at the same time thy
lies. And as for Zehowah, thinkest thou that she
would have loved thee, even if she had married thee?
I tell thee that her soul rejoices only in the light of the
faith, and that although she might have married thee,
she would have done so in the hope of turning thy
people from the worship of false gods and not for love of
thee. For she will never love any man." When I had
said this the soul groaned aloud and then remained
silent.

'In a little while the angel came back, and I saw
that his face was no longer clouded with anger. "Hear
the judgment of Allah," he said. "Inasmuch as thou
tookest the law upon thyself, which belonged to Allah
alone, thou deservest to die. But in so far as thou hast
indeed slain a hypocrite and an unbeliever thou hast
earned life. Allah is just, merciful and forgiving. It
is not meet that in thy lot there should be nothing but
reward or nothing but punishment. Therefore thou
shalt not yet receive a soul. Go hence to the third
heaven and when the angel Asrael shall be at leisure
he will write thy name in the book of the living. Then
thou shalt return hither and go into the city of Riad
bearing gifts. And Zehowah will accept thee in marriage,
though she love thee not, for Allah commands that it be

so. But if in the course of time this virtuous woman be moved to love, and say to thee, 'Khaled, I love thee,' then at that moment thou shalt receive an immortal soul, and if thy deeds be good thy soul shall enter paradise with the believers, but if not, thou shalt burn. Thus saith Allah. Thus art thou rewarded, indeed, but wisely and temperately, since thou hast not obtained life directly, but only the hope of life." Then the angel departed again, leading the way.

'But the soul mocked me. "Thou that sayest of Zehowah that she will never love any man, thou art fallen into thine own trap," it cried. "For now, if she love thee not thou must perish. Truly, Allah heard my prayer." But I was filled with thankfulness and departed after the angel, leaving the soul sitting alone upon the red sand.

'Thus have I told thee my history, O Asrael. And now I pray thee to write my name in the book of the living that I may fulfil the command of Allah and go my way to the city of Riad.'

Then Asrael again took up his pen to write in the book.

'Now thou art become a living man, though thou hast as yet no soul,' he said. 'And thou art subject to death by the sword and by sickness and by all those evils which spring up in the path of the living. And the day of thy death is already known to Allah who knows all things. But he is merciful and will doubtless grant thee a term of years in which to make thy trial. Nevertheless be swift in thy journey and speedy in all thou doest, for though mortal man may live for ever hereafter in glory, his years on earth are but as the breath which springs up in the desert towards evening and is gone before the stars appear.'

Khaled made a salutation before Asrael and went out of the third heaven, and passed through the second which is of burnished steel, and through the first in which the stars hang by golden chains, where Adam waits for the day of the resurrection, and at the gate he found the angel who had led him, and who now lifted him in his arms and bore him back to the Red Desert; for as he was now a mortal man he could no longer move through the air like the genii between the outer gate of heaven and the earth. Nor could he any longer see the soul of the Indian prince sitting upon the sand, though it was still there. But the angel was visible to him. So they stood together, and the angel spoke to him.

'Thou art now a mortal man,' he said, 'and subject to time as to death. To thee it seems but a moment since we went up together to the gate, and yet thou wast standing ten months and thirteen days before Asrael, and of the body of the man whom thou slewest only the bones remain.'

So saying the angel blew upon the red sand and Khaled saw the white bones of the prince in the place where he had laid his body. So he was first made conscious of time.

'Nearly a year has passed, and though Allah be very merciful to thee, yet he will assuredly not suffer thee to live beyond the time of other men. Make haste therefore and depart upon thine errand. Yet because thou art come into the world a grown man, having neither father nor mother nor inheritance, I will give thee what is most necessary for thy journey.'

Then the angel took a handful of leaves from a ghada bush close by and gave them to Khaled, and as he gave them they were changed into a rich garment, and into linen, and into a shawl with which to make a turban, and shoes of red leather.

'Clothe thyself with these,' said the angel.

He broke a twig from the bush and placed it in Khaled's hand. Immediately it became a sabre of Damascus steel, in a sheath of leather with a belt.

'Take this sword, which is of such fine temper that it will cleave through an iron headpiece and a shirt of mail. But remember that it is not a sword made by magic. Let thy magic reside in thy arm, wield it for the faith, and put thy trust in Allah.'

Afterwards the angel took up a locust that was asleep on the sand waiting for the warmth of the morning sun. The angel held the locust up before Khaled, and then let it fall. But as it fell it became at once a beautiful bay mare with round black eyes wide apart and an arching tail which swept down to the sand like a river of silk.

'Take this mare,' said the angel; 'she is of the pure breed of Nejed and as swift as the wind, but mortal like thyself.'

'But how shall I ride her without saddle or bridle?' asked Khaled.

'That is true,' answered the angel.

He laid leaves of the ghada upon the mare's back and they became a saddle, and placed a twig in her mouth and it turned into a bit and bridle.

Khaled thanked the angel and mounted.

'Farewell and prosper, and put thy trust in Allah, and forget not the day of judgment,' the angel said, and immediately returned to paradise.

So Khaled was left alone in the Red Desert, a living man obliged to shift for himself, liable to suffer hunger and thirst or to be slain by robbers, with no worldly possessions but his sword, his bay mare, and the clothes on his back. He knew moreover that he was more than two hundred miles from the city of Riad, and he knew that he could not accomplish this journey in less than four days. For when he was one of the genii he had often watched men toiling through desert on foot, and on camels and on horses, and had laughed with his companions at the slow progress they made. But now it was no laughing matter, for he had forgotten to ask the angel for dates and water, or even for a few handfuls of barley meal.

He turned the mare's head westward of the Goat, in which is the polar star, for he remembered that when he had carried away the Indian prince he had flown toward the south-east, and as he began to gallop over the dark sand he laughed to himself.

'What poor things are men and their horses,' he said. 'To destroy me, this mare need only stumble and lame herself, and we shall both die of hunger and thirst in the desert.'

This reflection made him at first urge the mare to her greatest speed, for he thought that the sooner he should be out of the desert and among the villages beyond, the present danger would be passed. But presently he bethought him that the mare would be more likely to stumble and hurt herself in the dark if she were galloping than if she were moving at a moderate pace. He therefore drew bridle and patted her neck and made her walk slowly and cautiously forward.

But this did not please him either, after a time, for he remembered that if he rode too slowly he must die of hunger before reaching the end of his journey.

'Truly,' he said, 'one must learn what it is to be a man, in order to understand the uses of moderation. Gallop not lest thy horse fall and thou perish! Nor delay walking slowly by the road, lest thou die of thirst and hunger! Yet thou art not safe, for Al Walid died from treading upon an arrow, and Oda ibn Kais perished by perpetual sneezing. Allah is just and merciful! I will let the mare go at her own pace, for the end of all things is known.'

The mare, being left to herself, began to canter and carried Khaled onward all night without changing her gait.

'Nevertheless,' thought Khaled, 'if we are not soon out of the desert we shall suffer thirst during the day as well as hunger.'

When there was enough daylight to distinguish a black thread from a white, Khaled looked before him and saw that there was nothing but red sand in hillocks and ridges, with ghada bushes here and there. But still the mare cantered on and did not seem tired. Soon the sun rose and it grew very hot, for the air was quite still and it was summer time.

Khaled looked always before him and at last he saw a white patch in the distance and he knew that there must be water near it. For the water of the Red Desert whitens the sand. He therefore rode on cheerfully, for he was now thirsty, and the mare quickened her pace, for she also knew that she was near a drinking-place. But as they came close to the spot Khaled remembered that the preceding night had been Al Kadr, which falls between the seventh and eighth latter days of the month Ramadhan, during which the true believers neither eat nor drink so long as there is light enough to distinguish a white thread from a black one. So, when they reached the well, he let his mare drink her fill, and he took off the saddle and bridle and let her loose, after which he sat down with his head in the shade of a ghada bush to rest himself.

'Allah is merciful,' he said; 'the night will come, and then I will drink.' For he dared not ride farther, for fear of not finding water again.

Then again he was disturbed, for he had nothing to eat, and he thought that if he waited until night he would be hungry as well as thirsty. But presently he saw the mare trying to catch the locusts that flew about. She could only catch one or two, because it was now hot and they were able to fly quickly.

'When the night comes,' he said, 'the locusts will lie on the ground and cling to the bushes, being stiff with the cold, and then I will eat my fill, and drink also.'

Soon afterwards he fell asleep, being weary, and when he awoke it was night again and the stars were shining overhead. Khaled rose hastily and drank at

the well and made ablutions and prayed, prostrating
himself towards the Kebla. He remembered that he
had slept a long time, and that he had not performed
his devotions for a day and a night, so that he repeated
them five times, to atone for the omission.

The mare was eating the locusts that now lay in
great black patches on the sand unable to move and
save themselves. Khaled threw his cloak over a great
number of them and gathered them together. Then he
kindled a fire of ghada by striking sparks from the
blade of his sword, and when he had made a bed of
coals he roasted the locusts after pulling off their legs,
and ate his fill. While he was doing this he was much
disturbed in mind.

'I have only just begun to live as a man,' he thought.
'Did I not stand ten months and thirteen days in the
third heaven, unconscious of the passing of time? Who
shall tell me whether I have not slept another ten
months or more under this bush, like the companions
of Al Rakim?'

So, when he had done eating and had drunk again
from the well, and had made the mare drink, he saddled
her quickly and mounted, and cantered on through the
night, guiding his course by the stars. On the following day he again found a well, but much later than
before, and he suffered much from thirst as he watched
his mare dip her black lips into the pool. Nevertheless

he would not break his fast, for he was resolved to be a true believer in practice as well as in belief. So he fell asleep and awoke when it was night again, and ate and drank. In this way he journeyed several days until he began to see the hill country which borders the desert towards Riad, and he understood that he had been much farther away than he had imagined. But he reflected that Allah had doubtless intended to try his constancy by imposing upon him the journey through the desert during the days of fasting. But at last, he awoke one day just at sunset, instead of sleeping until the night. He had been travelling up the first slopes where the ground, though barren, is harder than in the desert, and had lain down in a hollow by an abundant spring. He rose now and made ablutions and prayed, as usual, towards Mecca; that is to say, being where he was, he turned his face to the west as the sun was setting. When he had finished he stood some minutes watching the red light over the desert below him, and then he was suddenly aware that the new moon was hanging just above the diminishing fire of the evening, and he knew that the fast of Ramadhan was over and that the feast of Bairam had begun. Thereat he was glad, and determined to take an unusual number of locusts for his evening meal.

But when he looked about he saw that there were no locusts in the place, though there was grass, which his mare was eating. Then he looked everywhere near the well to see whether some traveller had not perhaps dropped a few dates or a little barley by accident, but there was nothing.

'Doubtless,' he said, 'Allah wishes to show me that greediness is a sin even on the day of feasting.'

He drank as much of the water as he could in order to stay his hunger as well as assuage his thirst, and then he saddled the mare and rode up out of the hollow towards the hill country. Towards the middle of the night he came to a small village where all the people were celebrating the feast, having killed a young camel and several sheep. Seeing that he was a traveller they bade him be welcome, and he sat down among them and ate his fill of meat, praising Allah. And corn was given to his mare, so that the dumb animal also kept the feast.

'Truly,' said the people, 'thy mare is a daughter of Al Borak, the heavenly steed called "the Lightning," upon which the nocturnal journey was accomplished by the Prophet, upon whom be peace.'

They said this not because they divined that the mare had been given to Khaled by an angel, but because they saw by her beauty that she must be swift as the wind. For she had a large head, with bony cheeks, and a full forehead and round black eyes wide apart, with smooth black skin about them, and a pointed nose,

and the under lip was like that of a camel, projecting a
little. And she was neither too long nor too short,
having straight legs like steel, and small feet and round
hoofs, neither overgrown in idleness nor overworn with
much work. And her tail lay flat and long and smooth
when she was standing still but arched like the plume
of an ostrich when she moved. Her coat was bright
bay, glossy and smooth and without any white mark-
ings. By all these signs, which belong to the purest
blood, the people of the village knew that she was
of the fleetest reared in Arabia. And Khaled was
glad that the people admired her, since she was the
chief of his few possessions, which indeed were not
many.

He did not know beforehand what he should do, nor
what he should say when in the presence of the Sultan
of Nejed, still less how he could venture to ask Zehowah
in marriage, having no gifts to offer and not being himself a prince. Before he had become a man it would
have been easy for him to find treasures in the earth
such as men had never seen, for, like all the genii, he
had been acquainted with the most deeply hidden
mines and with all places where men had hidden
wealth in old times. But this knowledge does not
belong to the intelligence becoming mortals, but rather
to the faculty of seeing through solid substance which
is exercised by the spirits of the air, and in his present

state it was taken from him, together with all possibility
of communicating with his former companions.   He
had nothing but his mare and his sword and the garments he wore, and though the mare was indeed a gift
for a king he did not know whether he was meant to
offer it to any one, seeing that it had been given him
by an angel.

Nevertheless he did not lose heart, for the celestial
messenger had told him that by the will of Allah he
should marry Zehowah, and Allah was certainly able to
give him a king's daughter in marriage without the
aid of gifts, of gold, of musk, of 'Ood, of aloes or of
pearls.

He rose, therefore, when he had eaten enough and
had rested himself and his mare, and after thanking the
people of the village for their entertainment he rode on
his way.   He passed through a hill country, sometimes
fertile and sometimes stony and deserted, but he found
water by the way and such food as he needed ; and
accomplished the remainder of the journey without
hindrance.

On the morning of the second day he came to a
halting-place from which he could see the city of Riad,
and he was astonished at the size and magnificence of
the Sultan's palace, which was visible above the walls
of the fortification.   Yet he was aware that he had seen
all this before as in a dream not altogether forgotten

when a man wakes at dawn after a long and restless
night.

He gazed awhile, after he had made his ablutions,
and then calling to his mare to come to him, he mounted
and rode through the southern gate into the heart of
the city.

CHAPTER II

WHEN Khaled reached the palace he dismounted from
his mare, and leading her by the bridle entered the
gateway.   Here he met many persons, guards, and
slaves both black and white, and porters bearing pro-
visions, and a few women, all hurrying hither and
thither ; and many noticed him, but a few gazed curiously into his face, and two or three grooms followed
him a little way, pointing out to each other the beauties
of his mare.

'Truly,' they said, 'if we did not know the mares of
the stud better than the faces of our mothers, we should
swear by Allah that this beast had been stolen from the
Sultan's stables by a thief in the night, for she is of the
best blood in Nejed.'

These being curious they saluted Khaled and asked
him whence he came and whither he was going, seeing
that it is not courteous to ask a stranger any other
questions.

'I come from the Red Desert,' Khaled answered, 'and
I am going into the palace as you see.'

The grooms saw that there was a rebuke in the last part of his answer and hung back and presently went their way.

'Are such mares bred in the Red Desert?' they exclaimed. 'The stranger is doubtless the sheikh of some powerful tribe. But if this be true, where are the men that came with him? And why is he dressed like a man of the city?'

So they hastened out of the gateway to find the Bedouins who, they supposed, must have accompanied Khaled on his journey.

But Khaled went forward and came to a great court in which were stone seats by the walls. Here a number of people were waiting. So he sat down upon one of the seats and his mare laid her nose upon his shoulder as though inquiring what he would do.

'Allah knows,' Khaled said, as though answering her. So he waited patiently.

At last a man came out into the courtyard who was richly dressed, and whom all the people saluted as he passed. But he came straight towards Khaled, who rose from his seat.

'Whence come you, my friend?' he inquired after they had exchanged the salutation.

'From the Red Desert, and I desire permission to speak with the Sultan when it shall please his majesty to see me.'

'And what do you desire of his majesty? I ask that I may inform him beforehand. So you will have a better reception.'

'Tell the Sultan,' said Khaled, 'that a man is here who has neither father nor mother nor any possessions beyond a swift mare, a keen sword and a strong hand, but who is come nevertheless to ask in marriage Zehowah, the Sultan's daughter.'

The minister smiled and gazed at Khaled in silence for a moment, but when he had looked keenly at his face, he became grave.

'It may be,' he thought, 'that this is some great prince who comes thus simply as in a disguise, and it were best not to anger him.'

'I will deliver your message,' he answered aloud, 'though it is a strange one. It is customary for those who come to ask for a maiden in marriage to bring gifts—and to receive others in return,' he added.

'I neither bring gifts nor ask any,' said Khaled. 'Allah is great and will provide me with what I need.'

'I fear that he will not provide you with the Sultan's daughter for a wife,' said the minister as he went away, but Khaled did not hear the words, though he would have cared little if he had.

Now it chanced that Zehowah was sitting in a balcony surrounded with lattice, over the courtyard, on that morning and she had seen Khaled enter, leading his mare by the bridle. But though she watched the stranger and his beast idly for some time she thought as little of the one as of the other, for her heart was not turned to love, and she knew nothing of horses. But her women thought differently and spoke loudly, praising the beauty of both.

'There is indeed a warrior able to fight in the front of our armies,' they said. 'Truly such a man must have been Khaled ibn Walad, the Sword of the Lord, in the days of the Prophet—upon whom peace.'

By and by there was a cry that the Sultan was coming into the room, and the women rose and retired. The Sultan sat down upon the carpet by his daughter, in the balcony.

'Do you see that stranger, holding a beautiful mare by the bridle?' he asked.

'Yes, I see him,' answered Zehowah indifferently.

'He is come to ask you in marriage.'

'Another!' she exclaimed with a careless laugh. 'If it is the will of Allah I will marry him. If not, he will go away like the rest.'

'This man is not like the rest, my daughter. He is either a madman or some powerful prince in disguise.'

'Or both, perhaps,' laughed Zehowah. She laughed often, for although she was not inclined to love, she was of a gentle and merry temper.

'His message was a strange one,' said the Sultan.

'He says that he neither brings gifts nor asks them, that he has neither father nor mother, nor any possessions excepting a swift mare, a keen sword and a strong hand.'

'I see the mare, the sword and the hand,' answered Zehowah. 'But the hand is like any other hand—how can I tell whether it be strong? The sword is in its sheath, and I cannot see its edge, and though the mare is pretty enough, I have seen many of your own I liked as well. The elephants of the Indian prince were more amusing, and the prince himself was more beautiful than this stranger with his black beard and his solemn face.'

'That is true,' said the Sultan with a sigh.

'Do you wish me to marry this man?' Zehowah asked.

'My daughter, I wish you to choose of your own free will. Nevertheless I trust that you will choose before long, that I may see my child's children before I die.'

For the Sultan was old and white-bearded, and was already somewhat bowed with advancing years and with burden of many cares and the fatigues of many wars. Yet his eye was bright and his heart fearless still, though his judgment was often weak and vacillating.

'Do you wish me to marry this man?' Zehowah asked again. 'He will be a strange husband, for he is a strange suitor, coming without gifts and having neither

father nor mother.   But I will do as you command.   If
you leave it to me I shall never marry.'

'I did not say that I desired you to take this one
especially,' protested the Sultan, 'though for the matter
of gifts I care little, since heaven has sent me wealth
in abundance.   But my remaining years are few,
and the years of life are like stones slipping from a
mountain which move slowly at first, and then faster
until they outrun the lightning and leap into the dark
valley below.   And what is required of a husband is
that he be a true believer, young and whole in every
part, and of a charitable disposition.'

'Truly,' laughed Zehowah, 'if he have no possessions,
charity will avail him little, since he has nothing to
give.'

'There is other charity besides the giving of alms,
my daughter, since it is charity even to think charitably
of others, as you know.   But I have not said that you
should marry this man, for you are free.   And indeed I
have not yet talked with him.   But I have sent for him
and you shall hear him speak.   See—they are just now
conducting him to the hall of audiences.   But indeed
I think he is no husband for you, after all.'

The Sultan rose and went to receive Khaled, and
Zehowah went to the secret window above her father's
raised seat in the hall.

Khaled made the customary salutation with the

greatest respect, and the Sultan made him sit down at his right hand as though he had been a prince, and asked him whence he had come. Then a refreshment was brought, and Khaled ate and drank a little, after which the Sultan inquired his business.

'I come,' said Khaled boldly, 'to ask your daughter Zehowah in marriage. I bring no gifts, for I have none to offer, nor have I any inheritance. My mare is my fortune, my sword is my argument and my wit is in my arm.'

'You are a strange suitor,' said the Sultan; but he kept a pleasant countenance, since Khaled was his guest. 'You are no doubt the sheikh of a tribe of the Red Desert, though I was not aware that any tribes dwelt there.'

'So far as being the sheikh of my tribe,' said Khaled with a smile, 'your majesty may call me so, for my tribe consists of myself alone, seeing that I have neither father nor mother nor any relations.'

'Truly, I have never talked with such a suitor before,' answered the Sultan. 'At least I presume that you are a son of some prince, and that you have chosen to disguise yourself as a rich traveller and to hide your history under an allegory.'

The Sultan would certainly not have allowed himself to overstep the bounds of courtesy so far, but for his astonishment at Khaled's daring manner. He was too keen, however, not to see that this man was something above the ordinary and that, whatever else he might be, he was not a common impostor. Such a fellow would have found means to rob a caravan of valuable goods, to offer as gifts, would have brought himself a train of camels and slaves and would have given himself out as a prince of some distant country from which it would not be possible to obtain information.

'Istaghfir Allah! I am no prince,' Khaled answered. 'I ask for the hand of your daughter. The will of Allah will be accomplished.'

He knew that Zehowah was watching and listening behind the lattice in her place of concealment, for the memory of such things had not been taken from him when he had lost the supernatural vision of the genii and had become an ordinary man. He was determined therefore to be truthful and to say nothing which he might afterwards be called upon to explain. For he never doubted but that Zehowah would be his wife, since the angel had told him that it should be so.

'And what if I refuse even to consider your proposal?' inquired the Sultan, to see what he would say.

'If it is the will of Allah that I marry your daughter, your refusal would be useless, but if it is not his will, your refusal would be altogether unnecessary.'

The Sultan was much struck by this argument which

showed a ready wit in the stranger and which he could only have opposed by asserting that his own will was superior to that of heaven itself.

'But,' said he, defending himself, 'any of the previous suitors might have said the same.'

' Undoubtedly,' replied Khaled, unabashed. ' But they did not say it. Your majesty will certainly now consider the matter.'

'In the meanwhile,' the Sultan answered, very graciously, 'you are my guest, and you have come in time to take part in the third day of the feast, to which you are welcome in the name of Allah, the merciful.'

Thereupon the Sultan rose and Khaled was conducted to the apartments set apart for the guests. But the Sultan returned to the harem in a very thoughtful mood, and before long he found Zehowah who had returned to her seat in the balcony.

' This is a very strange suitor,' he said, shaking his head and looking into his daughter's face.

' He is at least bold and outspoken,' she answered. ' He makes no secret of his poverty nor of his wishes. Whatever he be, he is in earnest and speaks truth. I would like well to know the only secret which he wishes to keep—who he really is.'

' It may be,' said the Sultan thoughtfully, ' that if I threaten to cut off his head he will tell us. But on the other hand, he is a guest.'

'He is not of those who are easily terrified, I think. Tell me, my father, do you wish me to marry him?'

'How could you marry a man who has no family and no inheritance? Would such a marriage befit the daughter of kings?'

'Why not?' asked Zehowah with much calmness.

The Sultan stared at her in astonishment.

'Has this stranger enchanted your imagination?' he inquired by way of answer.

'No,' replied Zehowah scornfully. 'I have seen the noblest, the most beautiful and the richest of the earth, ready to take me to wife, and I have not loved. Shall I love an outcast?'

'Then how can you ask my wishes?'

'Because there are good reasons why I should marry this man.'

'Good reasons? In the name of Allah let me hear them, if there are any.'

'You are old, my father,' said Zehowah, 'and it has not pleased heaven to send you a son, nor to leave you any living relation to sit upon the throne when your years are accomplished. You must needs think of your successor.'

'The better reason for choosing some powerful prince, whose territory shall increase the kingdom he inherits from me, and whose alliance shall strengthen the empire I leave behind me.'

'Istaghfir Allah! The worse reason. For such a prince would be attached to his own country, and would take me thither with him and would neglect the kingdom of Nejed, regarding it as a land of strangers whom he may oppress with taxes to increase his own splendour. And this is not unreasonable, since no king can wisely govern two kingdoms separated from each other by more than three days' journey. No man can have other than the one of two reasons for asking me in marriage. Either he has heard of me and desires to possess me, or he wishes to increase his dominions by the inheritance which will be mine.'

'Doubtless, this is the truth,' said the Sultan. 'But so much the more does this stranger in all probability covet my kingdom, since he has nothing of his own.'

'This is what I mean. For, having no other possessions to distract his attention, he will remain always here, and will govern your kingdom for its own advantage in order that it may profit himself.'

'This is a subtle argument, my daughter, and one requiring consideration.'

'The more so because the man seems otherwise well fitted to be my husband, since he is a true believer, and young, and fearless and outspoken.'

'But if this is all,' objected the Sultan, 'there are in Nejed several young men, sons of my chief courtiers, who possess the same qualifications. Choose one of them.'

' On the contrary, to choose one of them would arouse the jealousy of all the rest, with their families and slaves and freedmen, whereby the kingdom would easily be exposed to civil war.   But if I take a stranger it is more probable that all will be for him, since you are beloved, and there is no reason why one party should oppose him and another support him, since none of them know anything of him.'

' But he will not be beloved by the people unless he is liberal, and he has nothing wherewith to be generous.'

' And where are the treasures of Riad ?' laughed Zehowah.   ' Is it not easy for you to go secretly to his chamber and to give him as much gold as he needs ? '

' That is also true.   I see that you have set your heart upon him.'

' Not my heart, my father, but my head.   For I have infinitely more head than heart, and I see that the welfare of the kingdom will be better secured with such a ruler, than it would have been under a foreign prince whose right hand would be perpetually thrust out to take in Nejed that which his left hand would throw to courtiers in his own country.   Do I speak wisdom or folly ? '

' It is neither all folly nor all wisdom.'

' I have seen this man, I have heard him speak,' said Zehowah.   ' He is as well as another since I must

D

marry sooner or later. Moreover I have another argument.'

'What is that?'

'Either he is a man strong enough to rule me, or he is not,' Zehowah answered with a laugh. 'If he can govern me, he can govern the kingdom of Nejed. But if not I will govern it for him, and rule him also.'

The Sultan looked up to heaven and slightly raised his hands from his knees.

'Allah is merciful and forgiving!' he exclaimed. 'Is this the spirit befitting a wife?'

'Is it charity to cause happiness?'

'Undoubtedly it is charity.'

'And which is greater, the happiness of many or the happiness of one?'

'The happiness of many is greater,' answered the Sultan. 'What then?' he asked after a time, seeing that she said nothing more.

'I have spoken,' she replied. 'It is best that I should marry him.'

Then there was silence for a long time, during which the Sultan sat quite motionless in his place, watching his daughter, while she looked idly through the lattice at the people who came and went in the court below. She seemed to feel no emotion.

The Sultan did not know how to oppose Zehowah's will any more than he could answer her arguments, although his worldly wisdom was altogether at variance with her decision. For she was the beloved child of his old age and he could refuse her nothing. Moreover, in what she had said, there was much which recommended itself to his judgment, though by no means enough to persuade him. At last he rose from the carpet and embraced her.

'If it is your will, let it be so,' he said.

'It is the will of Allah,' answered Zehowah. 'Let it be accomplished immediately.'

With a sigh the Sultan withdrew and sent a messenger to Khaled requesting him to come to another and more secluded chamber, where they could be alone and talk freely.

Khaled showed no surprise on hearing that his suit was accepted, but he thought it fitting to express much gratitude for the favourable decision. Then the Sultan, who did not wish to seem too readily yielding, began to explain to Khaled Zehowah's reasons for accepting a poor stranger, presenting them as though they were his own.

'For,' he said, 'whatever you may in reality be, you have chosen to present yourself to us in such a manner as would not have failed to bring about a refusal under any other circumstances. But I have considered that as it will be your destiny, if heaven grants you life, to rule my kingdom after me, you will in all likelihood

rule it more wisely and carefully, for having no other
cares in a distant country to distract your attention;
and because you have no relations you are the less
liable to the attacks of open or secret jealousy.'

The Sultan then gave him a large sum of money in
gold pieces, which Khaled gladly accepted, since he had
not even wherewithal to buy himself a garment for the
wedding feast, still less to distribute gifts to the courtiers and to the multitude. The Sultan also presented
him with a black slave to attend to his personal wants.

Khaled then sent for merchants from the bazar,
and they brought him all manner of rich stuffs, such as
he needed. There came also two tailors, who sat down
upon a matting in his apartment and immediately
began to make him clothes, while the black slave sat
beside them and watched them, lest they should steal
any of the gold of the embroideries.

When it was known in the palace that the Sultan's
only daughter was to be married at once, there were
great rejoicings, and many camels were slaughtered and
a great number of sheep, to supply food for so great a
feast. A number of cooks were hired also to help those
who belonged to the palace, for although the Sultan fed
daily more than three hundred persons, guests, travellers,
and poor, besides all the members of the household, yet
this was as nothing compared with the multitude to be
provided for on the present occasion.

Then it was that Hadji Mohammed, the chief of the cooks, sat down upon the floor in the midst of the main kitchen and beat his breast and wept. For the confusion was great so that the voice of one man could not be heard for the diabolical screaming of the many, and the cooks smote the young lads who helped them, and these, running to escape from the blows, fell against the porters who came in from outside bearing sacks of sugar, and great baskets of fruit and quarters of meat and skins of water, and bushels of meal and a hundred other things equally necessary to the cooking; and the porters, staggering under their burdens, fell between the legs of the mules loaded with firewood, that had been brought to the gate, and the dumb beasts kicked violently in all directions, while the slaves who drove them struck them with their staves, and the mules began to run among the camels, and the camels, being terrified, rose from the ground and began to plunge and skip like young foals, while more porters and more mules and more slaves came on in multitudes to the door of the kitchen. And it was very hot, for it was noontide, and in summer, and there were flies without number, and the dogs that had been sleeping in the shade sprang up and barked loudly and bit whomsoever they could reach, and all the men bellowed together, so that the confusion was extreme.

'Verily,' cried Hadji Mohammed, 'this is not a

kitchen but Yemamah, and I am not the chief of the
cooks, but the chief of sinners and fuel for hell.' So he
wept bitterly and beat his breast.

But at last matters mended, for there were many
who were willing to do well, so that when the time
came Hadji Mohammed was able to serve an honourable feast to all, though the number of the guests was
not less than two thousand.

But Khaled, having visited the bath, arrayed himself
magnificently and rode upon his bay mare to the
mosque, surrounded by the courtiers and the chief
officers of the state, and by a great throng of slaves
from the palace. As he rode, he scattered gold pieces
among the people from the bags which he carried, and
all praised his liberality and swore by Allah that
Zehowah was taking a very goodly husband. And as
none knew whence he came, all were equally pleased,
but most of all the Bedouins from the desert, of whom
there were many at that time in Riad, who had come to
keep the feast Bairam, for Khaled's own words had been
repeated, and they had heard that he came from the
desert like themselves. And when he had finished his
prayers, he rode back to the palace.

When the time for the feast came the Sultan led
Khaled into the great hall and made him sit at his right
hand. The Sultan himself was magnificently dressed
and covered with priceless jewels, so that he shone like

the sun among all the rest. Then he presented Khaled
to the assembly.

'This,' said he, 'is Khaled, my beloved son-in-law,
the husband of my only daughter, whom it has pleased
Allah to send me, as the stay of my old age and as the
successor to my kingdom. He will be terrible in war
as Khaled ibn Walid, his namesake, the Sword of the
Lord, and gentle and just in peace as Abu Bakr of
blessed memory. He is as brave as the lion, as strong
as the camel, as swift as the ostrich, as sagacious as the
fox and as generous as the pelican, who feeds her
young with the blood of her own breast. Love him
therefore, as you have loved me, for he is extremely
worthy of affection, and hate his enemies and be faithful
to him in the time of danger. By the blessing of Allah
he shall rear up children to me in my old age, to be
with you when he is gone.'

Thereupon Khaled turned and answered, speaking
modestly but with much dignity in his manner.

'Ye men of Nejed, this is my marriage feast and I
invite you all to be merry with me. Whether it shall
please Allah to give me a long life, or whether it shall
please him to take me this night I know not. We are
in the hand of Allah. But this I do know. I will love
you as my own people, seeing that I have no people of
my own. I will fight for you as a man fights for his
own soul, for his wife and for his children, and I will

divide justly the spoils in war, and give in peace whatsoever I am able, to all those who are in need. I swear
by Allah! You are all witnesses.'

The courtiers and all the guests were much pleased
with this short speech, for they saw that Khaled was a
man of few words and not proud or overbearing, and
none could look into his face and doubt his promise.
For the present moment at least Zehowah's prediction
had been verified, for no one was jealous of him, and
there was but one party among them all and that was
for him. So they all feasted together in harmony until
the sun was low.

In the meantime Zehowah remained in the harem,
surrounded by her women, and a separate meal was
brought to them. They all sat upon the rich carpets
leaning on cushions set against the walls, and small
low tables were brought in, covered with dishes and
bowls containing delicately prepared rice and mutton
in great abundance and fresh blanket bread, hot from
the stones, and olives brought from Syria. Afterwards
came sweetmeats without number, such as Hadji
Mohammed knew how to prepare, and gold and silver
goblets filled with a drink made from large sweet
lemons and water, which is called 'treng.' Zehowah
indeed ate sparingly, for she was accustomed to such
dainties every day, but her women were delighted with
the abundance and left nothing to be taken away.

While they were eating six of the women played upon musical instruments by turns, while others danced slow and graceful measures, singing as they moved, and describing the unspeakable happiness which awaited their princess in marriage. Afterwards when the tables had been taken away and they had washed their hands with rose water from Ajjem, Zehowah commanded the singing and the dancing to cease, and the women brought her one by one the dresses which she was to wear before Khaled. They were very magnificent, for it had needed many years to prepare them, and a great weight of gold and silver threads had been weighed out to the tailors and embroiderers who had worked in the preparation of them ever since Zehowah had been two years old. For the piece of material is weighed first, and then the gold, and afterwards, when the work is finished, the whole is weighed together, lest the tailors should steal anything.

But Zehowah looked coldly at the garments, one after the other, as they were brought and taken away, and the women fancied that she was to be married to the stranger against her will, and that she remembered the Indian prince.

'It is a pity,' one of them ventured to say, 'that the bridegroom has not brought any elephants with him, for we would have watched them from the balconies, since they are diverting beasts.'

'And it is a pity,' said Zehowah scornfully, 'that my husband has not a round, soft face, like the moon in May, and the eyes of a gazelle and the heart of a hare. Truly, such a one would have made you a good king, seeing that he was also an unbeliever!'

'Nay,' said the woman humbly, 'Allah forbid that I should make a comparison, or bring an ill omen on the day by speaking of that which chanced a year ago. Truly, I only spoke of elephants, and not of men. For, surely, we all said when we saw him in the court that he looked a brave warrior and a goodly man.'

Then a messenger came from the Sultan saying that it was time to make ready. So they went to another apartment, where the nuptial chamber had been prepared. The Sultan came, then, leading Khaled, and followed by the Kadi, and all the women veiled themselves while the latter read the declaration of marriage. After that they all withdrew and Khaled took his seat upon the high couch in the middle of the room. Presently all the women returned, unveiled, with loud singing and playing of instruments, leading Zehowah dressed in the first of the dresses which she was to put on, and which, though it was very splendid, was of course the least magnificent of all those which had been prepared. But Khaled sat in his place looking on quietly, for he was acquainted with the custom, and he cared little for the rich garments, but looked always into Zehowah's face.

CHAPTER III

KHALED sat with his sword upon his feet, and when Zehowah was not in the room he played with the hilt and thought of all that was happening.

'Truly,' he said to himself, 'Allah is great. Was I not, but a few days since, one of the genii condemned to perish at the day of the resurrection? And am I not now a man, married to the most beautiful woman in the whole world, and the wisest and the best, needing only to be loved by her in order to obtain an undying soul? And why should this woman not love me? Truly, we shall see before long, when this mummery is finished.'

So he sat on the couch while Zehowah was led before him again and again each time in clothing more splendid than before, and each time with new songs and new music. But at the last time the attendants left her standing before him and went away, and only a very old woman remained at the door, screaming out in a cracked voice the customary exhortations. Then she, too, went away and the door was shut and Khaled and Zehowah were alone.

It was now near the middle of the night. The chamber was large and high, lighted by a number of hanging lamps such as are made in Bagdad, of brass perforated with beautiful designs and filled with coloured glasses, in each of which a little wick floats upon oil. Upon the walls rich carpets were hung, both Arabian and Persian, some taken in war as booty, and some brought by merchants in time of peace. A brass chafing dish stood at some distance from the couch, and upon the coals the women had thrown powdered myrrh and benzoin before they went away. But Khaled cared little for these things, since he had seen all the treasures of the earth in their most secret depositories.

Zehowah had watched him narrowly during the ceremony of the dresses and had seen that he felt no surprise at anything which was brought before him.

'His own country must be full of great wealth and magnificence,' she thought, 'since so much treasure does not astonish him.' And she was disappointed.

Now that they were alone, he still sat in silence, gazing at her as she stood beside him, and not even thinking of any speech, for he was overcome and struck dumb by her eyes.

'You are not pleased with what I have shown you,' Zehowah said at last in a tone of displeasure and disappointment. 'And yet you have seen the wealth of my father's palace.'

'I have seen neither wealth nor treasure, neither rich garments, nor precious stones nor chains of gold nor embroideries of pearls,' Khaled answered slowly.

But Zehowah frowned and tapped the carpet impatiently with her foot where she stood, for she was annoyed, having expected him to praise the beauty of her many dresses.

'They who have eyes can see,' she said. 'But if you are not pleased, my father will give me a hundred dresses more beautiful than these, and pearls and jewels without end.'

'I should not see them,' Khaled replied. 'I have seen two jewels which have dazzled me so that I can see nothing else.'

Zehowah gazed at him with a look of inquiry.

'I have seen the eyes of Zehowah,' he continued, 'which are as the stars Sirius and Aldebaran, when they are over the desert in the nights of winter. What jewels can you show me like these?'

Then Zehowah laughed softly and sat down beside her husband on the edge of the couch.

'Nevertheless,' she said, 'the dresses are very rich. You might admire them also.'

'I will look at them when you are not near me, for then my sight will be restored for other things.'

Khaled took her hand in his and held it.

'Tell me, Zehowah, will you love me?' he asked in a soft voice.

'You are my lord and my master,' she answered, looking modestly downward, and her hand lay quite still.

She was so very beautiful that as Khaled sat beside her and looked at her downcast face, and knew that she was his, he could not easily believe that she was cold and indifferent to him.

'By Allah!' he thought, 'can it be so hard to get a woman's love? Truly, I think she begins to love me already.'

Zehowah looked up and smiled carelessly as though answering his question, but Khaled was obliged to admit in his heart that the answer lacked clearness, for he found it no easier to interpret a woman's smile than men had found it before him, and have found it since, even to this day.

'You have had many suitors,' he said at last, 'and it is said that your father has given you your own free choice, allowing you to see them and hear them speak while he was receiving them. Tell me why you have chosen me rather than the rest, unless it is because you love me? For I came with empty hands, and without servants or slaves, or retinue of any kind, riding alone out of the Red Desert. It was therefore for myself that you took me.'

'You are right. It was for yourself that I took you.'

'Then it was for love of me, was it not?'

'There were and still are many and good reasons,' answered Zehowah calmly, and at the same time withdrawing her hand from his and smoothing back the black hair from her forehead. 'I told them all to my father, and he was convinced.'

'Tell them to me also,' said Khaled.

So she explained all to him in detail, making him see everything as she saw it herself. And the explanation was so very clear, that Khaled felt a cold chill in his heart as he understood that she had chosen him rather for politic reasons, than because she wished him for her husband.

'And yet,' she added at the end, 'it was the will of Allah, for otherwise I would not have chosen you.'

'But surely,' he said, somewhat encouraged by these last words, 'there was some love in the choice, too.'

'How can I tell!' she exclaimed, with a little laugh. 'What is love?'

Finding himself confronted by such an amazing question, Khaled was silent, and took her hand again. For though many have asked what love is, no one has ever been able to find an answer in words to satisfy the questioner, seeing that the answer can have no more to do with words than love itself, a matter sufficiently explained by a certain wise man, who understood the heart of man. If, said he, a man who loves a woman, or a woman who loves a man could give in words the precise reason why he or she loves, then love itself could be defined in language; but as no man or woman has ever succeeded in doing this, I infer that they who love best do not themselves know in what love consists—still less therefore can any one else know, wherefore the definition is impossible, and no one need waste time in trying to find it.

A certain wit has also said that although it be impossible for any man to explain the nature of love to many persons at the same time, he generally finds it easy to make his explanations to one person only. But this is a mere quibbling jest and not deserving of any attention.

Zehowah expected an answer to her question, and Khaled was silent, not because he was as yet too little acquainted with the feelings of a man to give them expression, but because he already felt so much that it was hard for him to speak at all.

Zehowah laughed and shook her head, for she was not of a timid temper.

'How can you expect me to say that I love you, when you yourself are unable to answer such a simple question?' she asked. 'And besides, are you not my lord and my master? What is it then to you, whether I love you or not?'

But again Khaled was silent, debating whether he should tell her the truth, how the angel had promised in

Allah's name that if she loved him he should obtain an undying soul, and how the task of obtaining her love had been laid upon him as a sort of atonement for having slain the Indian prince. But as he reflected he understood that this would probably estrange her all the more from him.

'Yet I can answer your question,' he said at last. 'What is love? It is that which is in me for you only.'

'But how am I to know what that is?' asked Zehowah, drawing up the smooth gold bracelets upon her arm and letting them fall down to her wrist, so that they jangled like a camel's bell.

'If you love me you will know,' Khaled answered, 'for then, perhaps, you will feel a tenth part of what I feel.'

'And why not all that you feel?' she asked, looking at him, but still playing with the bracelets.

'Because it is impossible for any woman to love as much as I love you, Zehowah.'

'You mean, perhaps, that a woman is too weak to love so well,' she suggested. 'And you think, perhaps, that we are weak because we sit all our lives upon the carpets in the harem eating sweetmeats, and listening to singing girls and to old women who tell us tales of long ago. Yet there have been strong women too—as strong as men. Kenda, who tore out the heart of Kamsa —was she weak?'

E

'Women are stronger to hate than to love,' said Khaled.

'But a man can forget his hatred in the love of a woman, and his strength also,' laughed Zehowah. ' I would rather that you should not love me at all, than that you should forget to be strong in the day of battle. For I have married you that you may lead my people to war and bring home the spoil.'

'And if I destroy all your enemies and the enemies of your people, will you love me then, Zehowah?'

'Why should I love you then, more than now? What has war to do with love? Again, I ask, what is it to you whether I love you or not? Am I not your wife, and are you not my master? What is this love of which you talk? Is it a rich garment that you can wear? A precious stone that you can fasten in your turban? A rich carpet to spread in your house? A treasure of gold, a mountain of ambergris, a bushel of pearls from Oman? Why do you covet it? Am I not beautiful enough?' Then is love henna to make my hair bright, or kohl to darken my eyes, or a boiled egg with almonds to smooth my face? I have all these things, and ointments from Egypt, and perfumes from Syria, and if I am not beautiful enough to please you, it is the will of Allah, and love will not make me fairer.'

'Yet love is beauty,' Khaled answered. 'For Kadijah was lovely in the eyes of the Prophet, upon whom be peace, because she loved him, though she was a widow and old.'

'Am I a widow? Am I old?' asked Zehowah with some indignation. 'Do I need the imaginary cosmetic you call love to smooth my wrinkles, to lighten my eyes, or to make my teeth white?'

'No. You need nothing to make you beautiful.'

'And for the matter of that, I can say it of you. You tell me that you love me. Is it love that makes your body tall and straight, your beard black, your forehead smooth, your hand strong? Would not any woman see what I see, whether you loved her or not? See! Is your hand whiter than mine because you love and I do not?'

She laughed again as she held her hand beside his.

'Truly,' thought Khaled, 'it is less easy than I supposed. For the heart of a woman who does not love is like the desert, when the wind blows over it, and there are neither tracks nor landmarks. And I am wandering in this desert like a man seeking lost camels.'

But he said nothing, for he was not yet skilled in the arguments of love. Thereupon Zehowah smiled, and resting her cheek upon her hand, looked into his face, as though saying scornfully, 'Is it not all vanity and folly?'

Khaled sighed, for he was disappointed, as a thirsty

man who, coming to drink of a clear spring, finds
the water bitter, while his thirst increases and grows
unbearable.

'Why do you sigh?' Zehowah asked, after a little
silence. 'Are you weary? Are you tired with the
feasting? Are you full of bitterness, because I do not
love you? Command me and I will obey. Are you
not my lord to whom I am subject?'

He did not speak, but she drew him to her, so that
his head rested upon her bosom, and she began to sing
to him in a low voice.

For a long time Khaled kept his eyes shut, listening to her voice. Then, on a sudden, he looked up, and
without speaking so much as a word, he clasped her in
his arms and kissed her.

Before it was day there was a great tumult in the
streets of Riad, of which the noise came up even to the
chamber where Khaled and Zehowah were sleeping.
Zehowah awoke and listened, wondering what had happened and trying to understand the cries of the distant
multitude. Then she laid her hand upon Khaled's
forehead and waked him.

'What is it?' he asked.

'It is war,' she answered. 'The enemy have surprised the city in the night of the feast. Arise and take
arms and go out to the people.'

Khaled sprang up and in a moment he was clothed

and had girt on his sword. Then he took Zehowah in his arms.

'While I live, you are safe,' he said.

'Am I afraid? Go quickly,' she answered.

At that time the Sultan of Nejed was at war with the northern tribes of Shammar, and the enemy had taken advantage of the month of Ramadhan, in which few persons travel, to advance in great numbers to Riad. During the three days' feast of Bairam they had moved on every night, slaying the inhabitants of the villages so that not one had escaped to bring the news, and in the daytime they had hidden themselves wherever they could find shelter. But in the night in which Khaled and Zehowah were married they reached the very walls of the city, and waiting until all the people were asleep, a party of them had climbed up upon the ramparts and had opened one of the gates to their companions after killing the guards.

Khaled found his mare and mounted her without saddle or bridle in his haste, then drawing his sabre he rode swiftly out of the palace into the confusion. The enemy with their long spears were driving the panicstricken guards and the shrieking people before them towards the palace, slaughtering all whom they overtook, so that the gutters of the streets were already flowing with blood, and the horses of the enemy stumbled over the bodies of the defenders. The whole multitude of the pursued and the pursuers were just breaking out of the principal street into the open space before the palace when Khaled met them, a single man facing ten thousand.

'I shall certainly perish in this fight,' he said to himself, 'and yet I shall not receive the reward of the faithful, since Allah has not given me a soul. Nevertheless certain of these dogs shall eat dirt before the rest get into the palace.'

So he pressed his legs to the bare sides of his mare and lifted up his sword and rode at the foe, having neither buckler, nor helmet, nor shirt of mail to protect him, but only his clothes and his turban. But his arm was strong, and it has been said by the wise that it is better to fall upon an old lion with a reed than to stand armed in the way of a man who seeks death.

'Yallah! The Sword of the Lord!' shouted Khaled, in such a terrible voice that the assailants ceased to kill for a moment, and the terrified guards turned to see whence so great a voice could proceed; and some who had seen Khaled recognised him and ran to meet him, and the others followed.

When the enemy saw a single man riding towards them across the great square before the palace, they sent up a shout of derision, and turned again to the slaughter of such of the inhabitants as could not extricate themselves.

'Shall one man stop an army?' they said. 'Shall a fox turn back a herd of hyænas?'

But when Khaled was among them they found less matter for laughter. For the sword was keen, the mare was swift to double and turn, and Khaled's hand was strong. In the twinkling of an eye two of the enemy lay dead, the one cloven to the chin, the other headless.

Then a strange fever seized Khaled, such as he had not heard of, and all things turned to scarlet before his eyes, both the walls of the houses, and the faces and the garments of his foes. Men who saw him say that his face was white and shining in the dawn, and that the flashing of the sword was like a storm of lightning about his head, and after each flash there was a great rain of blood, and a crashing like thunder as the horses and men of the enemy fell to the earth.

In the meantime, too, the soldiers of the city and the Bedouins of the desert who were within the walls for the feast, took courage, and turning fiercely began to drive the assailants back by the way they had come, towards the market-place in the bazar. But those behind still kept pressing forward, while those in front were driven back, and the press became so great that the Shammars could no longer wield their weapons. The enemy were crowded together like sheep in a fold, and Khaled, with his men, began to cut a broad road through the very midst of them, hewing them down in ranks and throwing them aside, as corn is harvested in Egypt.

But after some time Khaled saw that he was alone, with a few followers, surrounded by a great throng of the enemy, for some of his men had been slain after slaying many of their foes, and some had not been able to follow, being hindered at first by the heaps of dead and afterwards by the multitude of their opponents who closed in again over the bloody way through which Khaled had passed.

And now the Shammars saw that Khaled could not escape them, and they pressed him on every side, but the archers dared not shoot at him for fear of hitting their own friends, if their arrows chanced to go by the mark. Otherwise he would undoubtedly have perished, since he had no armour, and not even a buckler with which to ward off the darts. But they thrust at him with spears and struck at him with their swords, and wounded him more than once, though he was not conscious of pain or loss of blood, being hot with the fever of the fight. He was hard pressed therefore, and while he smote without ceasing he began to know that unless a speedy rescue came to him, his hour was at hand. From the borders of the market-place, the men of Riad could still see his sword flashing and striking, and they still heard his fierce cry.

He looked about him as he fought, and he saw that

he was now almost alone. One after another, the few
who had penetrated so far forward with him into the
press, were overwhelmed by numbers and fell bleeding
from a hundred wounds till only a score were left, and
Khaled saw that unless he could now cut his way free,
he must inevitably perish. But the press was stubborn
and a man might as well hope to make his way through
a herd of camels crowded together in a narrow street.
Then Khaled bethought him of a stratagem. He alone
was on horseback, for the enemy's riders had ridden
before, and he had met them in the street leading to the
palace, when he had himself slain many, and where the
rest were even now falling under the swords of the men
of Riad. And the few men who were with him were
also all on foot. Therefore looking across the market-
place he made as though he saw a great force coming
to his assistance, and he shouted with all his breath,
while his arm never rested.

'Smite, men of Nejed!' he cried. 'For I see the
Sultan himself coming to meet us with five hundred horsemen! Smite! Yallah! It is the Sword of the Lord!'

Hearing these words, his men were encouraged, and
of the enemy many turned their heads to see the new
danger. But being on foot they were hindered from
seeing by the throng. Yet so much the more Khaled
shouted that the Sultan was coming, and many of the
heads that turned to look were not turned back again,

but rolled down to the feet of those to whom they had
belonged. The brave men who were with Khaled took
heart and hewed with all their might, taking up the cry
of their leader when they saw that it disconcerted their
foes, so that the last took fright, and the panic ran
through the whole multitude.

'We shall be slain like sheep, and taken like locusts
under a mantle, for we cannot move!' they cried, and
they began to press away out of the market-place, forcing
their comrades before them into the narrow streets.

But here many perished. For while every man in
Riad had taken his sword and had gone out of his house
to fight, the women had dragged up cauldrons of boiling
water, and also hand-mill stones, to the roofs, and they
scalded and crushed their retreating foes. Then too, as
the market-place was cleared, the soldiers came on from
the side of the palace, having slain all that stood in
their way and taken most of their horses alive, which
alone was a great booty, for there are not many horses
in Nejed besides those of the Sultan, though these are
the very best and fleetest in all Arabia. But the Shammars of the north are great horse-breeders. So the
soldiers mounted and joined Khaled in the pursuit,
and a great slaughter followed in the streets, though
some of the enemy were able to escape to the gates, and
warn those of their fellows who were outside to flee to
the hills for safety, leaving much booty behind.

At the time of the second call to prayer Khaled dismounted from his mare in the market-place, and there was not one of the enemy left alive within the walls. Those who remember that day say that there were five thousand dead in the streets in Riad.

Khaled made such ablution as he could, and having prayed and given thanks to Allah, he went back on foot to the palace, his bay mare following him, and thrusting her nose into his hand as he walked. For she was little hurt, and the blood that covered her shoulders and her flanks was not her own. But Khaled had many wounds on him, so that his companions wondered how he was able to walk.

In the court of the palace the Sultan came to meet him, and fell upon his neck and embraced him, for many messengers had come, from time to time, telling how the fight went, and of the great slaughter. And Khaled smiled, for he thought that he should now win the love of Zehowah.

'Said I not truly that he is as brave as the lion, and as strong as the camel?' cried the Sultan, addressing those who stood in the court. 'Has he not scattered our enemies as the wind scatters the sand? Surely he is well called by the name Khaled.'

'Forget not your own men,' Khaled answered, 'for they have shared in the danger and have slain more than I, and deserve the spoil. There was a score of stout fellows with me at the last in the market-place, whose faces I should know again on a cloudy night. They fought as well as I, and it was the will of Allah that their enemies should broil everlastingly and drink boiling water. Let them be rewarded.'

'They shall every one have a rich garment and a sum of money, besides their share of the spoil. But as for you, my beloved son, go in and rest, and bind up your wounds, and afterwards there shall be feasting and merriment until the night.'

'The enemy is not destroyed yet,' answered Khaled. 'Command rather that the army make ready for the pursuit, and when I have washed I will arm myself and we will ride out and pursue the dogs until not one of them is left alive, and by the help of Allah we will take all Shammar and lay it under tribute and bring back the women captive. After that we shall feast more safely, and sleep without fear of being waked by a herd of hyænas in our streets.'

'Nay, but you must rest before going upon this expedition,' objected the Sultan.

'The true believer will find rest in the grave, and feasting in paradise,' answered Khaled.

'This is true. But even the camel must eat and drink on the journey, or both he and his master will perish.'

'Let us then eat and drink quickly, that we may the sooner go.'

'As you will, let it be,' said the Sultan, with a sigh, for he loved feasting and music, being now too old to go out and fight himself as he had formerly done.

Thereupon Khaled went into the harem and returned to Zehowah's apartment. As he went the women gathered round him with cries of gladness and songs of triumph, staunching the blood that flowed from his wounds with their veils and garments as he walked. And others ran before to prepare the bath and to tell Zehowah of his coming.

When she saw him she ran forward and took him by the hands and led him in, and herself she bathed his wounds and bound them up with precious balsams of great healing power, not suffering any of the women to help her nor to touch him, but sending them away so that she might be alone with Khaled.

'I have slain certain of your enemies, Zehowah,' he said, at last, 'and I have driven out the rest from the city.' As yet neither of them had spoken.

'Do you think that I have not heard what you have done?' Zehowah asked. 'You have saved us all from death and captivity. You are our father and our mother. And now I will bring you food and drink and afterwards you shall sleep.'

'So you are well pleased with the doings of the husband you have married,' he said.

He was displeased, for he had supposed that she

would love him for his deeds and for his wounds and that she would speak differently. But though she tended him and bound his wounds, and bathed his brow with perfumed waters, and laid pillows under his head and fanned him, as a slave might have done, he saw that there was no warmth in her cheek, and that the depths of her eyes were empty, and that her hands were neither hot nor cold. By all these signs he knew that she felt no love for him, so he spoke coldly to her.

'Is it for me to be pleased or displeased with the deeds of my lord and master?' she asked. 'Nevertheless, thousands are even now blessing your name and returning thanks to Allah for having sent them a preserver in the hour of danger. I am but one of them.'

'I would rather see a faint light in your eyes, as of a star rising in the desert than hear the blessings of all the men of Nejed. I would rather that your hand were cold when it touches mine, and your cheek hot when I kiss it, than that your father should bestow upon me all the treasures of Riad.'

'Is that love?' asked Zehowah with a laugh. 'A cold hand, a hot cheek, a bright eye?'

Khaled was silent, for he saw that she understood his words but not his meaning. It was now noon and it was very hot, even in the inner shade of the harem, and Khaled was glad to rest after the hard fighting, for his many slight wounds smarted with the healing balsam, and his heart was heavy and discontented.

Then Zehowah called a slave woman to fan him with a palm leaf, and presently she brought him meat and rice and dates to eat, and cool drink in a golden cup, and she sat at his feet while he refreshed himself.

'How many did you slay with your own hand?' she asked at last, taking up the good sword which lay beside him on the carpet.

CHAPTER IV

KHALED pondered deeply, being uncertain what to do, and trying to find out some action which could win for him what he wanted. Zehowah received no answer to her question as to the number of enemies he had slain and she did not ask again, for she thought that he was weary and wished to rest in silence.

'What do you like best in the whole world?' he asked after a long time, to see what she would say.

'I like you best,' she answered, smiling, while she still played with his sword.

'That is very strange,' Khaled answered, musing. But the colour rose darkly in his cheeks above his beard, for he was pleased now as he had been displeased before.

'Why is it strange?' asked Zehowah. 'Are you not the palm tree in my plain, and a tower of refuge for my people?'

'And will you dry up the well from which the tree draws life, and take away the corner-stone of the tower's foundation?'

'You speak in fables,' said Zehowah, laughing.

'Yet you imagined the fable yourself, when you likened me to a palm and to a tower. But I am no lover of allegories. The sword is my argument, and my wit is in my arm. The wall by the tree is the wall of love, and the chief foundation of the tower is the love of Zehowah. If you destroy that, the tree will wither and the tower will fall.'

'Surely there was never such a man as you,' Zehowah answered, half jesting but half in earnest. 'You are as one who has bought a white mare; and though she is fleet, and good to look at, and obedient to his voice and knee, yet he is discontented because she cannot speak to him, and he would fain have her black instead of white, and if possible would teach her to sing like a Persian nightingale.'

'Is it then not natural in a woman to love man? Have you heard no tales of love from the story-tellers of the harem?'

'I have heard many such tales, but none of them were told of me,' Zehowah replied. 'Will you drink again? Is the drink too sweet, or is it not cool?'

She had risen from her seat and held the golden cup, bending down to him, so that her face was near his. He laid his hand upon her shoulder.

'Hear me, Zehowah,' he said. 'I want but one thing in the world, and it was for that I came out of the Red

Desert to be your husband. And that thing I will
have, though the price be greater than rubies, or than
blood, or than life itself.'

'If it is mine, I freely give it to you. If it is not
mine, take it by force, or I will help you to take it by
a stratagem, if I can. Am I not your wife?'

She spoke thus, supposing from his face that he meant
some treasure that could be taken by strength or by
wile, for she could not believe a man could speak so
seriously of a mere thought such as love.

'Neither my right hand nor your wit can give me
this, but only your heart, Zehowah,' he answered, still
holding her and looking at her.

But now she did not laugh, for she saw that he was
greatly in earnest.

'You are still talking of love,' she said. 'And you
are not jesting. I do not know what to answer you.
Gladly will I say, I love you. Is that all? What is it
else? Are those the words?'

'I care little for the words. But I will have the
reality, though it cost your life and mine.'

'My life? Will you take my life, for the sake of a
thought?'

'A thought!' he exclaimed. 'Do you call love a
thought? I had not believed a woman could be so
cold as that.'

'If not a thought, what then? I have spoken the

truth. If it were a treasure, or anything that can be taken, you could take it, and I could help you. But if the possibility of possessing it lie not in deeds, it lies in thoughts, and is itself a thought. If you can teach me, I will think what you will ; but if you cannot teach me, who shall ? And how will it profit you to take my life or your own ? '

' Is it possible that love is only a thought ? ' asked Khaled, speaking rather to himself than to her.

' It must be,' she answered. ' The body is what it is in the eyes of others, but the soul is what it thinks itself to be, happy or unhappy, loving or not loving.'

' You are too subtle for me, Zehowah,' Khaled said. ' Yet I know that this is not all true.'

For he knew that he possessed no soul, and yet he loved her. Moreover he could think himself happy or unhappy.

' You are too subtle,' he repeated. ' I will take my sword again and I will go out and fight, and pursue the enemy and waste their country, for it is not so hard to cut through steel as to touch the heart of a woman who does not love, and it is easier to tear down towers and strongholds of stone with the naked hands than to build a temple upon the moving sand of an empty heart.'

Khaled would have risen at once, but Zehowah took his hand and entreated him to stay with her.

' Will you go out in the heat of the day, wounded

and wearied?' she asked. 'Surely you will take a
fever and die before you have followed the Shammars
so far as two days' journey.'

'My wounds are slight, and I am not weary,' Khaled
answered. 'When the smith has heated the iron in
the forge, does he wait until it is cold before striking?'

'But think also of the soldiers, who have striven
hard, and cannot thus go out upon a great expedition
without preparation as well as rest.'

'I will take those whom I can find. And if they
will go with me, it is well. But if not, I will go alone,
and they and the rest will follow after.'

'It is summer, too,' said Zehowah, keeping him back.
'Is this a time to go out into the northern desert?
Both men and beasts will perish by the way.'

'Has not Allah bound every man's fate about his
neck? And can a man cast it from him?'

'I know not otherwise, but if heat and hunger and
thirst do not kill the men, they will certainly destroy
the beasts, whose names are not recorded by Asrael, and
who have no destiny of their own.'

'You hinder me,' said Khaled. 'And yet you do
not know how many of the Shammar may be yet lurking within a day's march of the city, slaying your
people, burning their houses and destroying their har-
vest. Let me go. Will you love me better if I stay?'

'You will be the better able to get the victory.'

'Will you love me better if I stay?'

'If you go now, you may fail in your purpose and perish as well. How could I love you at all then?'

'It is the victory you love then—not me?'

'Could I love defeat? Nay, do not be angry with me. Stay here at least until the evening. Think of the burning sun and the raging thirst and the smarting of your wounds which have only been dressed this first time. Think of the soldiers, too——'

'They can bear what I can bear. Was it not summer-time when the Prophet went out against the Romans?'

'I do not know. Stay with me, Khaled.'

'I will come back when I have destroyed the Shammars.'

'And if the soldiers will not go with you, will you indeed go out alone?'

'Yes. I will go alone. When they see that they will follow me. They are not foxes. They are brave men.'

Khaled rose and girt his sword about him. Zehowah helped him, seeing that she could not persuade him to stay.

'Farewell,' he said, shortly, and without so much as touching her hand he turned and went out. She followed him to the door of the room and stood watching as he went away.

'One of us two was to rule,' she said to herself, 'and

it is he, for I cannot move him. But what is this talk
of love? Does he need love, who is himself the master?'

She sighed and went back to the carpet on which
they had been sitting. Then she called in her women
and bid them tell her all they had heard about the fight
in the morning; and they, thinking to please her, ex-
tolled the deeds of Khaled and of the tens he had slain
they made hundreds, and of the thousands of the
enemy's army, they made tens of thousands, till the
walls of Riad could not have contained the hosts of
which they spoke, and the dry sand of the desert could
not have drunk all the blood which had been shed.

Meanwhile Khaled went into the outer court of
the palace, where many soldiers were congregated together in the shade of the high wall, eating camel's
meat and blanket bread and drinking the water from the
well. They were all able-bodied and unhurt, for those
who had been wounded were at their houses, tended by
their wives.

'Men of Riad!' cried Khaled, standing before them.
'We have fought a good fight this morning and the
power of our foes is broken. But all are not yet destroyed, and it may be that there are many thousands
still lurking within a day's march of the city, slaying
the people, burning their houses and destroying their
harvests. Let us go out and kill them all before they
are able to go back to their own country. Afterwards

we will pursue those who are already escaping, and we will lay all the tribes of Shammar under tribute and bring back the women captive.'

Thereupon a division arose among the soldiers. Some were for going at once with Khaled, but others said it was the hot season and no time for war.

'It is indeed summer,' said Khaled. 'But if the Shammars were able to come to Riad in the heat, the men of Riad are able to go to them. And I at least will go at once, and those who wish to share the spoil will go with me, but those who are satisfied to sit in the shade and eat camel's meat will stay behind. In an hour's time I will ride out of the northern gate.'

So saying, Khaled rode slowly down into the city towards the market-place. The people were carrying away their own dead, and dragging off the bodies of their enemies, with camels, by fours and fives tied together to bury them in a great ditch without the walls. When Khaled appeared, many of the men gathered round him, with cries of joy, for they had supposed that some of his wounds were dangerous and that they should not see him for many days.

'Wallah! He is with us again!' they shouted, jostling each other to get near, and standing on tiptoe to see the good mare that had carried him so well in the fight.

'Masallah! I am with you,' answered Khaled, 'and if you will go with me we will send many more of the

Shammars to eat thorns and thistles, as many as dwell
in Kasim and Tabal Shammar as far as Haïl; and by
the help of Allah we will take the city of Haïl itself
and divide the spoil and bring away the women captive;
and when we have taken all that there is we will lay
the land under tribute and make it subject to Nejed.
So let those who will go with me arm themselves and
take every man his horse or his camel, and dates and
barley and water-skins, and in an hour's time we will
ride out. For Allah will certainly give us the victory.'

'Let us bury the dead to-day and to-morrow we will
go,' said many of those nearest to him.

'Are there no old men and boys in Riad to bind the
sheaves you have mown?' asked Khaled. 'And are
there no women to mourn over the dead of your kindred
who have fallen in a good fight? And as for to-morrow,
it is yet in Allah's hand. But to-day we have already
with us. However, if you will not go with me, I will
go alone.'

The men were pleased with Khaled's speech, and
indeed the greater part of the dead were buried by this
time, for all the people had made haste to the work,
fearing lest the bodies should bring a pestilence among
them, since it was summer-time and very hot. Then
all those who were unhurt and could bear arms, went
and washed themselves, and took their weapons and
food, as Khaled had directed them. Before the call to

afternoon prayers the whole host went out of the northern gate.

Then Khaled accomplished all that he had spoken of, and much more, for he drove the scattered force of the enemy before him, overtaking all at last and slaying all whom he overtook as far as Zulfah which is by the narrow end of the Nefud. Here he rested a short time, and then quickly crossing the sand, he entered the country called Kasim which is subject to the Shammars. Here he was told by a woman who had been taken that the Shammars were coming with a new army against him out of Haïl. He therefore hid his host in a pass of the hills just above the plain, and sent down a few Bedouins to encamp at the foot of the mountains, bidding them call themselves Shammars and make a show of being friendly to the enemy. So when the army of the Shammars reached the foot of the hills, they saw the tents and only one or two camels, and Khaled's Bedouins came out and welcomed them, and told them that Khaled was still crossing the Nefud, and that if they made haste through the hills they might come upon him unawares and at an advantage as he began to ascend. Thereupon the enemy rejoiced and entered the pass in haste, after filling their water-skins.

When they were in the midst of the hills, Khaled and his army sprang up from the ambush and fell upon them, and utterly destroyed them, taking all their

horses and camels and arms ; after which he went down
into the plain and laid waste the country about Haïl.
He took the city as the Shammars had taken Riad.
For he himself got upon the wall at night, with the
strongest and the bravest of his followers, and slew the
guards and opened the gate just before the dawn. But
there was no Khaled in Haïl to rally the soldiers and
give them heart to turn and make a stand in the streets.

Khaled then entered the palace and took the Sultan
of Shammar alive, not suffering him to be hurt, for he
wished to bring him to Riad. This Sultan was a man of
middle age, having only one eye, and also otherwise ill-
favoured, besides being cowardly and fat. So Khaled
ordered that he should be put into a litter, and the
litter into a cage, and the cage slung between two
camels. But he commanded that the women of the
harem should be well treated and brought before him,
that he might see them, intending to bring back the
most beautiful of them as presents to his father-in-law.

'Surely,' said the men who were with him, 'you will
keep the fairest for yourself.'

But Khaled turned angrily upon them.

'Have I not lately married the most beautiful woman
in the world ?' he asked. 'I tell you it is for her sake
that I have destroyed the Shammars. But the Sultan
shall have the best of these women, and afterwards the
rest of them will be divided amongst you by lot.'

When the women heard that they were to be distributed among the men of Nejed they at first made a pretence of howling and beating their breasts, but they rejoiced secretly and soon began to laugh and talk among themselves, pointing out to each other the strongest and most richly dressed of Khaled's followers, as though choosing husbands among them. But one of them neither wept nor spoke to her companions, but stood silently watching Khaled, and when he sat down upon a carpet in the chief kahwah of the house, she brought him drink in a goblet set with pearls from Katar, and sat down at his feet as though she had been his wife. But he took little heed of her at first, for he was busy with grave matters.

The other women, seeing what she did, thought that she was acting wisely in the hope of gaining Khaled's favour, seeing that he was the chief of their enemies, so they, too, came near, and brought water for his hands, and perfumes, and sweetmeats, thinking to outdo her. But she pushed them away, taking what they brought for him, and offering it herself.

'Are you better than we?' the women said angrily. 'Has our lord chosen you for himself, that you will not let us come near him?'

Then Khaled noticed her and began to wonder at her attention and zeal.

'What is your name?' he asked. But she did

not speak. 'Who is she?' he inquired of the other women.

'She is an unbeliever,' they answered contemptuously. 'And she is proud, for she trusts in her white skin and her blue eyes, and her hair which is red without henna. She thinks she is better than we. Command us to uncover our faces, that you may see and judge between us.'

'Let it be so. Let us see who is the fairest,' said Khaled, and he laughed.

Then the woman who sat at his feet threw aside her veil, and all the others did the same. Khaled saw that the one was certainly more beautiful than the rest, for her skin was as white as milk, and her eyes like the sea of Oman when it is blue in winter. She had also long hair, plaited in three tresses which came down to her feet, red as the locusts when the sun shines upon them at evening, and not dyed.

'There is a bay mare in a stable of black ones,' Khaled said. 'What is the name of the bay mare?'

'Her name is Aziz, and she is a Christian,' said one of the women.

'Not Aziz—Almasta,' said the beautiful woman in an accent which showed that she could not speak Arabic fluently. 'Almasta, a Christian.'

'She was lately sent as a present to our master by the Emir of Basrah,' said one of the others.

'He paid a thousand and five hundred sequins for her, for she was brought from Georgia,' said another. 'But I am a free woman, and myself the daughter of an emir.'

Then all the others began to scream.

'It is a lie,' they cried. 'Your father was a white slave from Syria.'

'You are fools,' retorted the woman who had spoken. 'You should have said that you were also free women and the daughters of emirs. So our lord would have treated you with more consideration.'

The others saw their folly and were silent and drew back, but Khaled only smiled.

'As good mares are bred in the stable as in the desert,' he said, and the women laughed with him at the jest, for they saw that it pleased him.

But Almasta was silent and sat at his feet, looking into his face.

'You must learn to talk in Arabic,' he said, 'and then you will be able to tell stories of your native country to the Sultan, for he loves tales of travel.'

Almasta smiled and bent her head a little, but she did not understand all he said, being but lately come into Arabia.

'I will go with you,' she answered.

'Yes. You will go with me to Riad to the Sultan, and perhaps he will make you his wife, for he has none at present.'

'I will go with you,' she repeated, looking at him.

'She does not understand you,' said the women, laughing at her ignorance of their own tongue.

'It is no matter,' said Khaled. 'She will learn in due time. Perhaps it has pleased Allah to send my lord the Sultan a wife without a tongue for a blessing in his old age.'

'I will go with you,' Almasta said again.

'She can say nothing else,' jeered the women.

One of them pulled her by her upper garment, so that she looked round.

'Can you say this, "My father was a dog and the son of dogs"?' asked the woman.

But Almasta pushed her angrily away, for she half understood. Then the woman grew angry too, and shook her fist in Almasta's face.

'If you fight, you shall eat sticks,' said Khaled, and then they were all quiet.

Thus he took possession of the city of Haïl and remaining there some time he reduced all the country to submission, so that it remained a part of the kingdom of Nejed for many years after that. For the power of the Shammars was broken, and they could nowhere have mustered a thousand men able to bear arms. Khaled set a governor in the place of the Sultan and ordered all the laws of the country in the same manner as those of Nejed, and after he had been absent from Riad nearly two months,

he set aside a part of his force to remain behind and
keep the peace in case there should be an outbreak,
and with the rest he began to journey homeward, taking
a great spoil and many captives with him.

During the march most of the women captives rode
on camels, but a few of the most beautiful were taken
in litters lest the fatigues of riding should injure their
appearance and thus diminish their value.   Almasta
was one of these, and the Sultan of Haïl was taken in a
cage as has been said, though he was not otherwise ill-
treated, and received his portion of camel's meat and
bread, equal to that of the soldiers.

Khaled sent messengers on fleet mares to Riad to
give warning of his coming, but he could not himself
proceed very quickly, because his army was burdened
with so much spoil ; and as there was now no haste to
overtake an enemy he journeyed chiefly at night, resting
during the day wherever there was water, for although
the summer was far advanced it was still hot.   He
thought continually of Zehowah, by day in his tent and
by night on the march, for he supposed that she would
be glad when she heard of the victory and that she
would now love him, because he had avenged her people,
and taken Haïl, and brought back gold and captives,
besides other treasures.

'She was already pleased with my deeds, before we
left Riad,' he thought, ' for she asked me how many of

the Shammars I had slain with my own hand, and at the last she wished me to stay with her, most probably that I might tell her more about the fight. How much the more will she be glad now, since I have killed so many more and have brought back treasure, and made a whole country subject to her father. Shall not blood and gold buy the love of a woman ? '

It chanced once during this journey that Khaled was sitting at the door of his tent after the sun had gone down and before the night march had begun. Upon the one side, at a little distance, was the tent of the women captives who had been taken from the palace in Haïl, and upon the other the soldiers had set down the cage in which the Sultan of Shammar was carried. The men had laid a carpet over the cage to keep the sun from the prisoner during the heat of the day, lest he should not reach Riad alive as Khaled desired. For the Sultan was fat and of a choleric temper. Now the soldiers had given him food but had forgotten to bring him water, and it was hot under the carpet now that the evening had come. But he could lift it up a little on one side, and having done so, he began to cry out, cursing Khaled and railing at him, not knowing that he was so near at hand.

' Oh you whose portion it shall be to broil everlastingly, and to eat thistles and thorns, and to lie bound in red-hot chains as I lie in this cage ! Have you brought me out into the desert to die of thirst like a lame camel? Surely your entertainment on the day of judgment shall be boiling water and the fruit of Al Zakkam, and whenever you try to get out of hell you shall be dragged back again and beaten with iron clubs, and your skin shall dissolve, and the boiling water shall be poured upon your head!'

In this way the captive cried out, for he was very thirsty. But when Khaled saw that no one gave him water he called in the darkness to the women who sat by their tent.

'Fetch water and give the man to drink,' he said.

One of the women rose quickly and filled a jar at the well close by, and took it to the cage. But then the railing and cursing broke out afresh, so that Khaled wondered what had happened.

'Who has sent me this unbelieving woman to torture me with thirst?' cried the prisoner. 'Are you not Aziz whom I was about to take for my fourth wife on account of your red hair? But your hair shall be a perpetual flame hereafter, burning the bones of your head, and your flesh shall be white with heat as iron in a forge. If I were still in my kingdom you should eat many sticks! If Allah delivers me from my enemies I will cause your skin to be embroidered with gold for a trapping to my horse!'

The moon rose at this time, being a little past the

full, and Khaled looked towards the cage and saw that the woman was standing two paces away from the Sultan's outstretched hand. She dabbled in the cool water with her fingers so that a plashing sound was heard, and then drank herself, and scattered afterwards a few drops in the face of the thirsty captive.

'It is good water,' she said. 'It is cold.'

Khaled knew from her broken speech that it was Almasta, and he understood that she was torturing the prisoner with the sound and sight of the water, and with her words. So he rose from his place and went to the cage.

'Did I not tell you to give him drink?' he asked, standing before the woman.

'Oh my lord, be merciful,' cried the captive, when he saw that Khaled himself was there. 'Be merciful and let me drink, for your heart is easily moved to pity, and by an act of charity you shall hereafter sit in the shade of the tree Sedrat and drink for ever of the wine of paradise.'

'I do not desire wine,' said Khaled. 'But you shall certainly not thirst. Give him the jar,' he said to Almasta. But she shook her head.

'He is bad and ugly,' she said. 'If he does not drink, he will die.'

Then Khaled put out his hand to take the jar of water, but Almasta threw it violently to the ground,

and it broke to pieces. Thereupon the captive began
again to rail and curse at Almasta and to implore
Khaled with many blessings.

'You shall drink, for I will bring water myself,' said
Khaled. He went back to his tent and took his own
jar to the well, and filled it carefully.

When he turned he saw that Almasta was running
from his tent towards the cage, with a drawn sword in
her hand. He then ran also, and being very swift of
foot, he overtook her just as she thrust at the Sultan
through the bars. But the sword caught in the folds of
the soft carpet, and Khaled took it from her hand, and
thrust her down so that she fell upon her knees. Then
he gave the prisoner the jar with the water that
remained in it, for some had been spilt as he ran.

'Who has given you the right to kill my captives?'
he asked of Almasta.

'Kill me, then!' she cried.

'Indeed, if you were not so valuable, I would cut off
your head,' Khaled answered. 'Why do you wish me
to kill you?'

'I hate him,' she said, pointing to the captive who
was drinking like a thirsty camel.

'That is no reason why I should kill you. Go back
to the tents.'

But Almasta laid her hand on the sword he held
and tried to bring it to her own throat.

'This is a strange woman,' said Khaled. 'Why do you wish to die? You shall go to Riad and be the Sultan's wife.'

'No, no!' she cried. 'Kill me! Not him, not him!'

'Of whom do you speak?'

'Him!' she answered, again pointing to the prisoner. 'Is he not the Sultan?'

Khaled laughed aloud, for he saw that she had supposed she was to be taken to Riad to be made the wife of the Sultan of Shammar. Indeed, the other women had told her so, to anger her.

'Not this man,' he said, endeavouring to make her understand. 'There is another Sultan at Riad. The Sultan of Shammar is one, the Sultan of Nejed another.'

'You?' she asked, suddenly springing up. 'With you?'

The moon was bright and Khaled saw that her eyes gleamed like stars and her face grew warm, and when she took his hands her own were cold.

'No, not I,' he answered. 'I am not the Sultan.'

But her face became grey in the moonlight, and she covered her head with her veil and went slowly back to her tent.

'This woman loves me,' Khaled thought. 'And as I have not talked much with her, it must be because I am strong and have conquered the people among whom she was captive. How much the more then, will Zehowah love me, for the same reason.'

So he was light of heart, and soon afterwards he commanded everything to be made ready and mounted his bay mare for the night march.

CHAPTER V

WHEN Khaled was within half a day's march of Riad,
the Sultan came out to meet him with a great train of
attendants and courtiers, with cooks bringing food and
sweetmeats, and a number of musicians. And they all
encamped together for a short time in the shade of the
trees, for there were gardens in the place. The Sultan
embraced Khaled and put upon him a very magnificent
garment, after which they sat down together in a large
tent which the Sultan had brought with him. When
they had eaten and refreshed themselves they began to
talk, and Khaled told his father-in-law all that he had
done, and gave him an account of the spoils which he
had brought back, commanding the most valuable
objects to be brought into the tent. After this the
Sultan desired to see the women captives.

'There is one especially whom it may please you to
take for yourself,' said Khaled, and he ordered Almasta
to be brought in.

When the male slaves had left the tent, Almasta
drew aside her veil. The Sultan looked at her

and smiled, stroking his beard, for he was much pleased.

'Her face is like a pearl and her hair is a setting of red gold,' he said. 'Truly she is like the sunrise on a fair morning when there are red clouds in the east.'

Almasta looked attentively at him, and afterwards she glanced at Khaled, who could not avoid looking at her on account of her beauty. Her face was grave and indifferent. Then Khaled told the Sultan how she had hated the Sultan of Shammar and had tried to kill him on the journey.

'This is a dangerous woman, my son,' said the old man. But he laughed as he said it, for although he was old, he was no coward. 'She is dangerous, indeed. Will you love me, pearl of my soul's treasures?' he inquired of her, still smiling.

'You are my lord and my master,' she answered, looking down.

When Khaled heard this he wondered whether his father-in-law would get any affection from her. Zehowah had answered in the same words.

'By Allah, I will give you such gifts as will make you love me,' said the Sultan. 'What shall I give you?'

'His head,' answered Almasta, raising her eyes quickly.

'The head of the Sultan of Shammar?'

Almasta nodded, and Khaled could see that her lips trembled.

'A dead man has no companions,' said the Sultan, looking at Khaled to see what he would do. But Khaled cared little, and said nothing.

So the Sultan called a slave and ordered the captive's head to be struck off immediately. Then Almasta threw herself upon the carpet on the floor of the tent and embraced his feet.

'See how easily the love of a woman is got,' Khaled thought, 'even by an old man whose beard is grey and his limbs heavy.'

When Almasta rose again, she looked at Khaled triumphantly, as though to remind him of the night on the journey when he had hindered her from killing the captive in his cage. But though he understood her, he held his peace, for he had cared nothing whether the prisoner lived or died after he had delivered him over to his father-in-law, and he was considering whether he might not please Zehowah in some similar manner. This was not easy, however, for he was not aware that Zehowah had any private enemy, whose head he might offer her.

After the Sultan had seen the other women and the best of the spoils, Khaled begged that he might be allowed to ride on into Riad alone, for he saw that the Sultan intended to spend the night in feasting where he had encamped. The Sultan was so much pleased with

Almasta and so greatly diverted in examining the rich stuffs and the gold and silver vessels and jewels, that he let Khaled go, almost without trying to detain him, though he made him many speeches praising his conduct of the war, and would have loaded him with gifts. But Khaled would take nothing with him, saying that he would only receive his just share with the rest; and the fame of his generosity immediately went abroad among the soldiers and the Bedouins throughout all the camp.

'For,' said Khaled, 'there is not a fleeter mare than mine among all those we have taken; my sword proves to be a good one, for I have tried it well; as for women, I am satisfied with one wife; and besides a wife, a sword and a horse, there are no treasures in the world which I covet.'

So Khaled rode away alone into Riad, for he desired no company, being busy with his own thoughts. He reached the gates at nightfall and went immediately to the palace and entered Zehowah's apartments. He found her sitting among her women in her accustomed place, listening to the tales of an old woman who sat in the midst of the circle. As soon as Zehowah saw her husband she sprang up gladly to meet him, as a friend would have done.

'Though it is summer-time, I have pursued the enemy,' said Khaled. 'And though the sun was hot, I have got the victory and brought home the spoil.'

He said this remembering how she had tried to hinder him from going. Then he gave her his sword and he sat down with her, while the women brought food and drink, for he was weary, and hungry and thirsty. The women also brought their musical instruments and began to sing songs in praise of Khaled's deeds; but after a time he sent them all away and remained alone with Zehowah.

'O Zehowah,' he said, 'you are my law and my rule. You are my speech and my occupation. You are my Kebla to which I turn in prayer. For the love of you I have got the victory over many foes. And yet I see that your cheek is cold and the light of your eyes is undisturbed. Have you no other enemies for me to destroy, or have you no secret foe whose head would be a pleasant gift?'

Zehowah laughed, as she fanned him with a palm leaf.

'Do you still thirst for war, Khaled?' she asked. 'Truly you have swallowed up all our enemies as the dry sand swallows up water. Where shall I find enemies enough for you to slay? You went out in pride and you have returned in glory. Are you not yet satisfied? And as for any secret foe, if I have any I do not know him. Rest, therefore; eat and drink and spend your days in peace.'

'I care little for either food or drink,' Khaled answered, 'and I need little rest.'

'Will nothing but war please you? Must you overcome Egypt and make Syria pay tribute as far as
Damascus before you will rest?'

'I will conquer the whole world for you, if you wish
it,' said Khaled.

'What should I do with the world?' asked Zehowah.
'Have I not treasures and garments enough and to spare,
besides the spoil you have now brought home? And
besides, if you would conquer the world you must needs
make war upon true believers, amongst whom we do
not count the people of Shammar. Be satisfied therefore and rest in peace.'

'How shall I be satisfied until I have kindled the
light in Zehowah's eyes at my coming, and until I feel
that her hand is cold and trembles when I take it in
mine?'

'Do I say to my eyes, "be dull"—or to my hand, "do
not tremble"?' Zehowah asked. 'Is this, which you
ask of me, something I can command at will, as I
can a smile or a word? If it is, teach me and I will
learn. But if not, why do you expect of me what I
cannot do? Can a camel gallop like a horse, or a horse
trot like a camel, or bear great burdens through the
desert? Have you come back from a great war only
to talk of this something which you call love, which is
yours and not mine, which you feel and I cannot feel,
which you cannot explain nor describe, and which, after

all, is but a whim of the fancy, as one man loves sour drink and another sweet?'

'Do you think that love is nothing but a whim of the fancy?' asked Khaled bitterly.

'What else can it be? Would you love me if you were blind?'

'Yes.'

'And if you were deaf?'

'Yes.'

'And if you could not touch my face with your hands, nor kiss me with your lips?'

'Yes.'

Zehowah laughed.

'Then love is indeed a fancy. For if you could not see me, nor touch me, nor hear me, what would remain to you but an empty thought?'

'Have I seen you, or touched you, or heard your voice for these two months and a half?' asked Khaled. 'Yet I have loved you as much during all that time.'

'You mean that you have thought of me, as I have thought of you, by the memory of what was not fancy, but reality. Would you dispute with me, Khaled? You will find me subtle.'

'There is more wit in my arm than in my head,' Khaled answered, 'and it is not easy for a man to persuade a woman.'

'It is very easy, provided that the man have reason

on his side. But where are the treasures you have
brought back, the slaves and the rich spoils? I would
gladly see some of them, for the messengers you sent
told great tales of the riches of Haïl.'

'To-morrow they will be brought into the city.
Your father has remained feasting in the gardens
towards Dereyiyah, and the whole army with him. I
rode hither alone.'

'Why did you not remain too?'

'Because that whim of the fancy which I call love
brought me back,' Khaled answered.

'Then I am glad you love me,' said Zehowah. 'For
I am glad you came quickly.'

'Are you truly glad?'

'I was very tired of my women,' she answered. 'I
am sorry you have brought nothing with you. Are
there any among the captives who are beautiful?'

'There is one, a present sent lately to the Sultan of
Shammar. She is very beautiful, and unlike all the
rest. Your father is much pleased with her, and will
perhaps marry her.'

'Of what kind is her beauty?' asked Zehowah.

'She is as white as milk, her eyes are twin sapphires,
her mouth is a rose, her hair is like gold reddened in
fire.'

Zehowah was silent for a while, and twisted a string
of musk-beads round her fingers.

'The others are all Arabian women,' Khaled said at last.

'Why did you not keep the beautiful one for yourself?' asked Zehowah, suddenly throwing aside her beads and looking at him curiously. 'Surely you, who have borne the brunt of the war, might have chosen for yourself what pleased you best.'

Khaled looked at her in great astonishment.

'Have I not married Zehowah? Would you have me take another wife?'

'Why not? Is it not lawful for a man to take four wives at one time? And this woman might have loved you, as you desire to be loved.'

'Would it be nothing to you, if I took her?'

'Nothing. I am the King's daughter. I shall always be first in the house. I say, she might love you. Then you would be satisfied.'

'Zehowah, Zehowah!' cried Khaled. 'Is love a piece of gold, that it matters not whence it be, so long as a man has it in his own possession? Or is it wood of the 'Ood tree that one may buy it and bring it home and make the whole house fragrant with it? Is a man's heart like his belly, which is alike satisfied with different kinds of food?'

'He who eats, knows by the taste whether he eats Persian mutton, or barley bread, or only broiled locusts. But a man who believes that he is loved, knows that he is loved, so far as knowing is possible, and must be satisfied, if to be loved is what he desires.'

'That may be true. But he who desires bread is not satisfied with locusts. It is your love which I would have. Not the love of another.'

'You are like a man who hopes to get by argument a sum of money from one who has nothing,' said Zehowah, smiling at him. 'Can you make gold grow in the purse of a beggar? Or can you cause a ghada bush to bear dates by reasoning with it? Your heart is a palm tree, but mine is a ghada bush.'

'Yet an angel may touch the ghada and it will bear fruit,' answered Khaled, for he remembered how the angel had turned dry leaves into rich garments for him to wear.

'Doubtless, Allah can do all things. But where is the angel? Hear me, Khaled, for I speak very reasonably, as a wife should speak to her husband, who is her lord and master. My lord is not satisfied with me and desires something of me which is not mine to give. Let him take another wife beside me. I have given my lord a kingdom and great riches and power. Let him take another wife now, who will give him this fancy of his thoughts for which he yearns, though she have no other possessions. In this way my lord will be satisfied.'

Khaled listened sadly to what Zehowah said, and he

began to despair, for he was not subtle in argument nor
eloquent in speech. The reason of this was plain. In
the days when he had been one of the genii he had
wandered over the whole earth and had heard the
eloquence of all nations and the arguments of all
philosophers, learning therefrom that deeds are no part
of words, and that they who would be believed must
speak little and do much. But the genii possess no
insight into the hearts of women.

Khaled reflected also that the length of life granted
him was uncertain, and that he had already spent two
months and a half at a distance from Zehowah in
accomplishing the conquest whereby he had hoped to
win her love. But since this had utterly failed, he cast
about in his mind for some new deed to do, which could
be done without leaving her even for a short time.
But he was troubled by her indifference, and most of
all by her proposing that he should take another wife.
As he thought of this, he was filled with horror, and he
understood that he loved Zehowah more than he had
supposed, since he could not bear to think of setting
another woman beside her.

Then his face became very dark and his eyes were
like camp fires far off in the desert, and he took
Zehowah's wrist in his hand, holding it tightly as
though he would not let it go. As his heart grew hot
in his breast, words came to his lips unawares like the

speech of a man in a dream, and he heard his own voice as it were from a distance.

'I will not take another,' he said. 'What is the love of any other woman to me? It is as dust in the throat of a man thirsting for water. Show me a woman who loves me. Her face shall be but a cold mirror in which the image of a fire is reflected without warmth, her soft words shall be to me as the screaming of a parrot, her touch a thorn and her lips ashes. What is it to me if all the women of the world love me? Kindle a fire and burn them before me, for I care not. Let them perish all together, for I shall not know that they are gone. I love you and not another. Shall it profit a man to fill his mouth with dust, though it be the dust of gold mingled with precious stones, when he desires water? Or shall he be warmed in winter by the reflection of a fire in a mirror? By Allah! I want neither the wealth of Haïl, nor a wife with red hair. Let them take gold who do not ask for love. I want but one thing, and Zehowah alone can give it to me. Wallah! My heart burns. But I would give it to be burned for ever in hell if I might get your love now. This I ask. This only I desire. For this I will suffer and for this I am ready to die before my time.'

Zehowah was silent, looking at him with wonder, and yet not altogether pleased. She saw that she could not understand him, though she did as well as she could.

'Has he not all that the heart of man can desire?'
she thought. 'Am I not young and beautiful, and
possessed of many jewels and treasures? Have I not
given him wealth and power, and has he not with his
own hand got the victory over his enemies and mine?
And yet he is not satisfied. Surely, he is too hard to
please.'

But he, reading her thoughts from her face, continued
in his speech.

'What is all the happiness of the world without
love?' he asked. 'It is like a banquet in which many
rich viands are served, but the guests cannot eat them
because there is no salt in any of them. And what is
a beautiful woman without love? She is like a garden
in which there are all kinds of rare flowers, and much
grass, and deep shade, but in which a man cannot live,
because nothing grows there which he can eat when he
is hungry.'

'Truly,' said Zehowah, 'that is what you will make
of your life. For there is a garden called Irem, planted
in a secret place of the deserts about Aden, by Sheddad
the son of Ad, who desired to outdo the gardens of
paradise, and was destroyed for his impiety with all his
people, by the hand of Allah. But a certain man
named Abdullah ibn Kelabah was searching in the
desert for a lost camel, and came unawares upon this
place. There were fruits and water there and all that

a man could wish for, and Abdullah dwelt in peace and
plenty, praising Allah.   Then on a certain day he
desired to eat an onion, and finding none anywhere, he
went out, intending to obtain one, and having eaten it,
to return immediately.   But though he searched the
desert many months he was never able to find the
garden again.   Wherefore it is said that Abdullah ibn
Kelabah lost the earthly paradise of Irem for a mouth-
ful of onion.'

'How can you understand me if you do not love
me?' asked Khaled. 'Love has its own language, and
when two love they understand each the other's words.
But when the one loves and the other loves not, they
are strangers, though they be man and wife; or they are
like Persians and Arabians not understanding either the
other's speech, or that if the wife cries "father," her
husband will bring her a cup of water supposing her to
be thirsty. For those who would speak one language
must be of one heart, and they who would be of one
heart must love each other.'

Then Zehowah sighed and leaned against the cushions
by the wall and drew her hand away from Khaled.

'What is it?' she asked in a low voice.   'What is it
you would have?' But though she had already asked
the question many times she found no answer, and none
that he was able to give could enlighten her darkness.

'It is the spark that kindles the flame,' Khaled said,

and he pointed to the lights that hung in the room.
'Your beauty is like that of a cunningly designed lamp,
inlaid with gold and silver and covered with rich ornament, which is seen by day. But there is no light
within, and it is cold, though it be full of oil and the
wick be ready.'

Zehowah turned towards him somewhat impatiently.

'And you are as one who would kindle the flame
with words, having no torch,' she answered.

'Have I not done deeds also?' asked Khaled. 'Or
have I spoken much, that you should reproach me?
Surely I have slain more of your enemies than I have
spoken words to you to-night.'

'But have I asked for an offering of blood, or a
marriage dower of dead bodies?'

Khaled was silent, for he was bitterly disappointed,
and as his eyes fell upon the sword which hung on the
wall, he felt that he could almost have taken it and
made an end of Zehowah for very anger that she would
not love him. Had he not gone out for her into the
raging heat of summer, and borne the burden of a great
war, and destroyed a nation and taken a city? Moreover, if neither words nor deeds could gain her love,
what means remained to him to try?

All through the night Khaled pondered, calling up
all that he had seen in the world in former times, until
he fell asleep at last, wearied in heart.

Very early in the morning one of Zehowah's women came and stood by his bed and waked him. He could see that her face was pale in the dawn, her limbs trembled and her voice was uncertain.

'Arise, my lord!' she said. 'A messenger has come from the army with evil news, and stands waiting in the court.'

Khaled sprang up, and Zehowah awoke also.

'What is this message?' he asked hastily.

But the woman threw herself upon the floor and covered her face, as though begging forgiveness because she brought evil tidings.

'Speak!' said Zehowah. 'What is it?'

'Our lord the Sultan is dead!' cried the woman, and she broke out into weeping and crying and would say nothing more.

But when Zehowah heard that her father was dead, she sat down upon the floor and beat her breast and tore her hair, and wailed and wept, while all the women of the harem came and gathered round her and joined in her mourning, so that the whole palace was filled with the noise of their lamentations.

Khaled went out into the court and questioned the messenger, who told him that the Sultan had held a great feast in the evening in the gardens of Dereyiyah, having with him the woman Almasta and the other captive women, and being served by black slaves. But,

suddenly, in the night, when most of the soldiers were
already asleep, there had been a great cry, and the
slaves and women had come running from the tent,
crying that the Sultan was dead. This was true, and
the Jewish physician who had gone out with his master
declared that he had died from an access of humours to
the head, brought on by a surfeit of sweetmeats, there
being at the time an evil conjunction of Zoharah and Al
Marech in square aspect to the moon and in the house
of death.

Khaled therefore mounted his bay mare and rode
quickly out to Dereyiyah, where he found that the news
was true, and the women were already preparing the
Sultan's body for burial. Having ordered the mourning,
and commanded the army to prepare for the return to the
city, Khaled set out with the funeral procession; and
when he reached the walls of Riad he turned to the left
and passed round to the north-east side of the city where
the burial-ground is situated. Here he laid the body
of his father-in-law in the tomb which the latter had
prepared for himself during his lifetime, and afterwards,
dismissing the mourners, he went back into the city
to the palace.

After the days of mourning were accomplished, the will
of the Sultan was made known, though indeed the people
were well acquainted with it already. By his will Khaled
succeeded to the sovereignty of the kingdom of Nejed

and to all the riches and treasures which the Sultan had accumulated during his lifetime. But the people received the announcement with acclamations and much joy, followed by a great feasting, for which innumerable camels were slain. Khaled also called all the chief officers and courtiers to a banquet and addressed them in a few words, according to his manner.

'Men of Nejed,' he said, 'it has pleased Allah to remove to the companionship of the faithful our master the Sultan, my revered father-in-law, upon whom be peace, and to set me up among you as King in his stead, being the husband of his only daughter, which you all know. As for the past, you know me; but if I have wronged any man let him declare it and I will make reparation. And if not, let none complain hereafter. But as for the future I will be a just ruler so long as I live, and will lead the men of Nejed to war, when there is war, and will divide the spoil fairly; and in peace I will not oppress the people with taxes nor change the just and good laws of the kingdom. And now the feast is prepared. Sit down cheerfully, and may Allah give us both the appetite to enjoy and the strength to digest all the good things which shall be set before us.'

But Khaled himself ate sparingly, for his heart was heavy, and when they had feasted and drunk treng juice and heard music, he retired to the harem, where he found Zehowah sitting with Almasta, the Georgian woman, there being no other women present in the room. He was surprised when he saw Almasta, though he knew that the captive women had been lodged in the palace, the distribution of the spoil from the war having been put off by the mourning for the Sultan.

When Almasta heard him enter, she looked up quickly and a bright colour rose in her face, as when the juice of a pomegranate is poured into milk, and disappeared again as the false dawn before morning, leaving no trace. Khaled sat down.

'Is not this the woman of whom you spoke?' Zehowah asked. 'I knew her from the rest by her red hair.'

'This is the woman. Your father would have taken her for his wife. But Allah has disposed otherwise.'

'She is beautiful. She is worthy to be a king's wife,' said Zehowah.

'The Sultan?' asked Almasta, for she hardly understood. Her face turned as white as bone bleached by the sun, and her fingers trembled, while her eyes were cast down.

Zehowah looked at Khaled and laughed.

'See how she trembles and turns pale before you,' she said. 'And a little while ago her face was red. You have found a torch wherewith to kindle this lamp, and a breath that can extinguish it.'

'I do not know,' Khaled answered. But he looked

attentively at Almasta and remained silent for some time. 'It is now necessary to divide the spoils of the war,' he said at last, 'and to bestow such of these women as you do not wish to keep upon the most deserving of the officers.'

'My lord will surely take the fairest for himself, since she loves him,' said Zehowah, again laughing, but somewhat bitterly.

'May my tongue be cloven and my eyes be put out, may my hands wither at the wrists and my feet fall from my ankles, if I ever take any wife but you,' said Khaled. 'Yallah! So be it.'

When Zehowah heard him say this, even while Almasta's face was unveiled before him, she understood that he was greatly in earnest.

'Let me keep her for my handmaid,' she said at last.

'Is she mine that you need ask me? But it will be wiser to give her to Abdul Kerim, the sheikh of the horsemen. I have promised that the spoil should be fairly divided, and though few have seen this woman many have heard of her beauty. And besides, she would weary you, for she cannot talk in Arabian, nor does she seem quick to learn. Abdul Kerim has the first right, since Allah has removed your father, upon whom be peace.'

'Your words are my laws,' answered Zehowah

obediently. 'And, indeed, it may be that you are right, for I believe she can neither dance nor sing, nor play upon any musical instrument. She would certainly weary me after a time, as you say. Give her therefore to Abdul Kerim for his share.'

They then made Almasta understand that she was to be given to the sheikh of the horsemen; but when she had understood she shook her head and smiled, though at first she said nothing, so that Khaled and Zehowah wondered whether she had comprehended what they had told her.

'Do you understand what we have told you?' asked Zehowah, who was diverted by her ignorance of the Arabic language.

'I understand.'

'And are you not pleased that you are to be the wife of Abdul Kerim, who is a rich man and still young?'

'I was to be the Sultan's wife,' said Almasta, with difficulty, looking at Khaled. 'You told me so.'

'The Sultan is dead,' Khaled answered.

'Who is the Sultan now?' she asked.

'Khaled is the Sultan,' said Zehowah.

'You said that I should be the Sultan's wife,' Almasta repeated.

'Doubtless, I said so,' Khaled replied. 'But Allah has ordered it otherwise.'

Almasta again smiled and shook her head.

CHAPTER VI

ON the following day Khaled made a division of the spoils, and gave Almasta to Abdul Kerim, enjoining upon him to marry her, since he had but two wives and could do so lawfully. The sheikh of the horsemen was glad, for he had heard much of Almasta's beauty, and he loved fair women, being of a fierce temper and not more than forty years old. So he called his friends to the marriage feast that same day, and Zehowah sent Almasta in a litter to his harem, giving her also numerous rich garments by way of a dower, but which in fact were due to Abdul Kerim as his share of the booty. So the men feasted, with music, until the evening, when the bridegroom retired to the harem and the Kadi came and read the contract; after which Abdul Kerim sat down while Almasta was brought before him in various dresses, one after the other, as is customary.

When the women were all gone away, Abdul Kerim began to talk to his wife, but she only laughed and said the few words she knew, not knowing what he said, and presently she began to sing to him in a low voice, in her own language. Her voice was very clear and quite different from that of the Arabian women whom Abdul had heard, and the tones vibrated with great passion and sweetness, so that he was enchanted and listened, as in a dream, while his head rested against Almasta's knee. She continued to sing in such a manner that his soul was transported with delight; and at last, as the sound soothed him, he fell into a gentle sleep.

Almasta, still singing softly, loosened his vest, touching him so gently that he did not wake. She then drew out of one of the three tresses of her hair a fine steel needle, extremely long and sharp, having at one end a small wooden ball for a handle, and while she sang, she thrust it very quickly into his breast to its full length, so that it pierced his heart and he died instantly. But she continued to sing, lest any of the women should be listening from a distance. Presently she withdrew the needle so slowly that not a drop of blood followed it, and having made it pass thrice through the carpet she restored it to her hair, after which she fastened the dead man's vest again, so that nothing was disarranged. She sang on, after this for some time, and then after a short silence she sprang up from the couch, uttering loud screams and lamentations and beating her breast violently.

The women of the harem came in quickly, and when

they saw that their master was dead, they sat down with Almasta and wept with her, for as he lay dead there was no mark of any violence nor any sign whereby it could be told that he had not died naturally.

When Khaled heard that Abdul Kerim was dead, he was much grieved at heart, for the man had been brave and had been often at his right hand in battle. But the news being brought to him at dawn when he awoke, he immediately sent the Jewish physician of the court to ascertain if possible the cause of the sudden death. The physician made careful examination of the body, and having purified himself returned to Khaled to give an account.

'I have executed my lord's orders with scrupulous exactness,' he said, 'and I find that without doubt the sheikh of the horsemen died suddenly by an access of humours to the heart, the sun being at that time in the Nadir, for he died about midnight, and being moreover in evil conjunction with the Dragon's Tail in the Heart of the Lion, and not yet far from the square aspect of Al Marech which caused the death of his majesty the late Sultan, upon whom be peace.'

But Khaled was thoughtful, for he reflected that this was the second time that a man had died suddenly when he was about to be Almasta's husband, and he remembered, how she had attempted to kill the Sultan of Haïl, and had ultimately brought about his death.

'Have you examined the dead man as minutely as you have observed the stars?' he inquired. 'Is there no mark of violence upon him, nor of poison, nor of strangling?'

'There is no mark. By Allah! I speak truth. My lord may see for himself, for the man is not yet buried.'

'Am I a jackal, that I should sniff at dead bodies?' asked Khaled. 'Go in peace.'

The physician withdrew, for he saw that Khaled was displeased, and he was himself as much surprised as any one by the death of Abdul Kerim, a man lean and strong, not given to surfeiting and in the prime of health.

'Min Allah!' he said as he departed. 'We are in the hand of the Lord, who knoweth our rising up and our lying down. It is possible that if I had seen this man at the moment of death, or a little before, I might have discovered the nature of his disease, for I could have talked with him and questioned him.'

But Khaled went in and talked with Zehowah. She was greatly astonished when she heard that Almasta's husband was dead, but she was satisfied with the answer of the Jewish physician, who enjoyed great reputation and was believed to be at that time the wisest man in Arabia.

'Give her back to me, to be one of my women,' said she. 'It is not written that she should marry a man of Nejed, unless you will take her yourself.'

But Khaled bent his brow angrily and his eyes glowed like the coals of a camp fire which is almost extinguished, when the night wind blows suddenly over the ashes.

'I have spoken,' he said.

'And I have heard,' she answered. 'Let there be an end. But give me this woman to divert me with her broken speech.'

'I fear she will do you an injury of which you may not live,' said Khaled.

'What injury can she do me?' asked Zehowah in astonishment, not understanding him.

'She asked of your father the head of the Sultan of Haïl, whom she hated. And your father gave it to her.'

'Peace be upon him!' exclaimed Zehowah piously.

'Upon him peace. And when he would have married her, he died suddenly at the feasting. And now this Abdul Kerim, who was to have been her husband, is dead also, without sign, in the night, as a man stung by a serpent in his sleep. These are strange doings.'

'If you think she has done evil, let her be put to death,' said Zehowah. 'But the physician found no mark upon Abdul Kerim. By the hand of Allah he was taken.'

'Doubtless his fate was about his neck. But it is strange.'

Zehowah looked at Khaled in silence, but presently she smiled and laid her hand upon his.

'This woman loves you with her whole soul,' she said. 'You think that she has slain Abdul Kerim by secret arts, in the hope that she may marry you.'

'And your father also.'

Then they were both silent, and Zehowah covered her face, since she could not prevent tears from falling when she thought of her father, whom she had loved.

'If this be so,' she said after a long time, 'let the woman die immediately.'

'It is necessary to be just,' Khaled answered. 'I will put no one to death without witnesses, not even a captive woman, who is certainly an unbeliever at heart. Has any one seen her do these deeds, or does any one know by what means a man may be slain in his sleep, or at a feast, so that no mark is left upon his body? At Dereyiyah your father was alone with her in the inner part of the tent, and she was singing to him that he might sleep. For I have made inquiry. And when Abdul Kerim died he was also alone with her. I cannot understand these things. But you are a woman and subtle. It may be that you can see what is too dark for me.'

'It may be. Therefore give her back to me, and I will lay a trap for her, so that she will betray herself if she has really done evil. And when we have convicted her by her own words she shall die.'

'Are you not afraid, Zehowah?'

'Can I change my destiny? If my hour is come, I shall die of a fever, or of a cold, whether she be with me or not. But if my years are not full, she cannot hurt me.'

'This is undoubtedly true,' answered Khaled, who could find nothing to say. 'But I will first question the woman myself.'

So he sent slaves with a litter to bring Almasta from the house of mourning to the palace, and when she was come he sent out all the other women and remained alone with her and Zehowah, making her sit down before him so that he could see her face. Her cheeks were pale, for she had not slept, having been occupied in weeping and lamentation during the whole night, and her eyes moved restlessly as those of a person distracted with grief.

Khaled then drew his sword and laid it across his feet as he sat and looked fixedly at Almasta.

'If you do not speak the truth,' he said, 'I will cut off your head with my own hand. Allah is witness.'

When Almasta saw the drawn sword, her face grew whiter than before, and for some moments she seemed not able to breathe. But suddenly she began to beat her breast, and broke out into loud wailings, rocking herself to and fro as she sat on the carpet.

'My husband is dead!' she cried. 'He was young;

I

he was beautiful! He is dead! Wah! Wah! my husband is dead! Kill me too!'

Khaled looked at Zehowah, but she said nothing, though she watched Almasta attentively. Then Khaled spoke to the woman again.

'Make an end of lamenting for the present,' he said. 'It has pleased Allah to take your husband to the fellowship of the faithful. Peace be upon him. Tell us in what manner he died, and what words he spoke when he felt his end approaching, for he was my good friend and I wish to know all.'

Almasta either did not understand or made a pretence of not understanding, but when she heard Khaled's words she ceased from wailing and sobbed silently, beating her breast from time to time.

'How did he die?' Khaled asked in a stern voice.

'He was asleep. He died,' replied Almasta in broken tones.

'You will get no other answer,' said Zehowah. 'She cannot speak our tongue.'

'Is there no woman among them all who can talk this woman's language?' asked Khaled with impatience, for he saw how useless it was to question her.

'There is no one. I have inquired. Leave her with me, and if there is anything to be known, I will try to find it out.'

So Khaled went away and Zehowah endeavoured to

soothe Almasta and make her talk in her broken words. But the woman made as though she would not be comforted, and went and sat apart upon the stone floor where there was no carpet, rocking to and fro, and wailing in a low voice. Zehowah understood that whatever the truth might be Almasta was determined to express her sorrow in the customary way, and that it would be better to leave her alone.

For seven days she sat thus apart, covering her head and mourning, and refusing to speak with any one, so that all the women supposed her to be indeed distracted with grief at the death of Abdul Kerim. And each day Khaled inquired of his wife whether she had yet learned anything, and received the same answer. But in the meantime he was occupied with his own thoughts, as well as with the affairs of the kingdom, though the latter were as nothing in his mind compared with the workings of his heart when he thought of Zehowah.

It chanced one evening that Khaled was riding among the gardens without the city, attended only by a few horsemen, for he was simple in all his ways and liked little to have a great throng of attendants about him. So he rode alone, while the horsemen followed at a distance.

'Was ever a man, or an angel, so placed in the world as I am placed?' he thought. 'How much better would it have been had I never seen Zehowah, and if I had

never slain the Indian prince. For I should still have
been with my fellows, the genii, from whom I am now
cut off, and at least I should have lived until the day
of the resurrection. But now my horse may stumble
and fall, and my neck may be broken, and there is no
hereafter. Or I may die in my sleep, or be killed in
my sleep, and there will be no resurrection for me, nor
any more life, anywhere in earth or heaven. For
Zehowah will never love me. Was ever a man so
placed? And I am ashamed to complain to her any
more, for she is a good wife, obedient and careful of
my wants, and beautiful as the moon at the full, rising
amidst palm trees, besides being very wise and subtle.
How can I complain? Has she not given me herself,
whom I desired, and a great kingdom which, indeed, I did
not desire, but which no man can despise as a gift? Yet
I am burned up within, and my heart is melting as a piece
of frankincense laid upon coals in an empty chamber,
when no man cares for its sweet savour. Surely, I am
the most wretched of mankind. Oh, that the angel who
made garments for me of a ghada bush, and a bay mare
of a locust, would come down and lay his hand upon
Zehowah's breast and make a living heart of the stone
which Allah has set in its place!'

So he rode slowly on, reasoning as he had often
reasoned before, and reaching the same conclusion in
all his argument, which availed him nothing. But sud-

denly, as the sun went down, a new thought entered his mind and gave him a little hope.

'The sun is gone down,' he said to himself. 'But Allah has not destroyed the sun. It will rise in the east to-morrow when the white cock crows in the first heaven. Many things have being, which the sight of man cannot see. It may be that although I see no signs of love in the heaven of Zehowah's eyes, yet love is already there and will before long rise as the sun and illuminate my darkness. For I am not subtle as the evil genii are, but I must see very clearly before I am able to distinguish.'

He rode back into the city, planning how he might surprise Zehowah and obtain from her unawares some proof that she indeed loved him. To this end he entered the palace by a secret gate, covering his garments with his aba, and his head with the kefiyeh he wore, in order to disguise himself from the slaves and the soldiers whom he met on his way to the harem. He passed on towards Zehowah's apartment by an unlighted passage not generally used, and hid himself in a niche of the wall close to the open door, from which he could see all that happened, and hear what was said.

Zehowah was seated in her accustomed place and Almasta was beside her. Khaled could watch their faces by the light of the hanging lamps, as the two women talked together.

'You must put aside all mourning now,' Zehowah
was saying. 'For I will find another husband for you.'

'Another husband?' Almasta smiled and shook her
head.

'Yes, there are other goodly men in Riad, though
Abdul Kerim was of the goodliest, as all say who knew
him. He was the Sultan's friend, but he was more
soldier than courtier. He deserved a better death.'

'Abdul Kerim died in peace. He was asleep.'
Almasta smiled still, but more sadly, and her eyes were
cast down.

'He died in peace,' Zehowah repeated, watching her
narrowly. 'But it is better to die in battle by the
enemy's hand. Such a man, falling in the front of the
fight for the true faith, enters immediately into paradise,
to dwell for ever under the perpetual shade of the tree
Sedrat, and neither blackness nor shame shall cover his
face. There the rivers flow with milk and with clarified
honey, and he shall rest on a couch covered with thick
silk embroidered with gold, and shall possess seventy
beautiful virgins whose eyes are blacker than mine and
their skin whiter than yours, having colour like rubies
and pearls, and their voices like the song of nightin-
gales in Ajjem, of which travellers tell. These are the
rewards of the true believer as set forth in Al Koran by
our prophet, upon whom peace. A man slain in battle
for the faith enters directly into the possession of all

this, but unbelievers shall be taken by the forelock and
the heels and cast into hell, to drink boiling molten
brass, as a thirsty camel drinks clear water.'

Almasta understood very little of what Zehowah
said, but she smiled, nevertheless, catching the meaning
of some of the words.

' The Sultan Khaled loves black eyes,' she said.   ' He
will go to paradise.'

'Doubtless, he will quench his thirst in the incor-
ruptible milk of heavenly rivers,' Zehowah replied.
' He is the chief of the brave, the light of the faith and
the burning torch of righteousness.   Otherwise Allah
would not have chosen him to rule.   But I spoke of
Abdul Kerim.'

' He died in peace,' said Almasta the second time,
and again looking down.

' I do not know how he died,' Zehowah answered,
looking steadily at the woman's face.   ' It was a great
misfortune for you.   Do you understand ?   I am very
sorry for you.   You would have been happy with Abdul
Kerim.'

' I mourn for him,' Almasta said, not raising her
eyes.

' It is natural and right.   Doubtless you loved him
as soon as you saw him.'

Almasta glanced quickly at Zehowah, as though
suspecting a hidden meaning in the words, and for a

moment each of the women looked into the other's eyes, but Zehowah saw nothing. For a wise man has truly said that one may see into the depths of black eyes as into a deep well, but that blue eyes are like the sea of Oman in winter, sparkling in the sun as a plain of blue sand, but underneath more unfathomable than the desert.

Almasta was too wise and deceitful to let the silence last. So when she had looked at Zehowah and understood, she smiled somewhat sorrowfully and spoke.

'I could have loved him,' she said. 'I desire no husband now.'

'That is not true,' Zehowah answered quickly. 'You wish to marry Khaled, and that is the reason why you killed Abdul Kerim.'

Almasta started as a camel struck by a flight of locusts.

'What is this lie?' she cried out with indignation. 'Who has told you this lie?' But her face was as grey as a stone, and her lips trembled.

'You probably killed him by magic arts learned in your own country,' said Zehowah quietly. 'Do not be afraid. We are alone, and no one can hear us. Tell me how you killed him. Truly it was very skilful of you, since the physician, who is the wisest man in Arabia, could not tell how it was done.'

But Almasta began to beat her breast and to make

oaths and asseverations in her own language, which Zehowah could not understand.

'If you will tell me how you did it, I will give you a rich gift,' Zehowah continued.

But so much the more Almasta cried out, stretching her hands upwards and speaking incomprehensible words. So Zehowah waited until she became quiet again.

'It may be that Khaled will marry you, if you will tell me your secret,' Zehowah said, after a time.

Then Almasta's cheek burned and she bent down her eyes.

'Will you tell me how to kill a man and leave no trace?' asked Zehowah, still pressing her. 'Look at this pearl. Is it not beautiful? See how well it looks upon your hair. It is as the leaf of a white rose upon a river of red gold. And on your neck—you cannot see it yourself—it is like the full moon hanging upon a milky cloud. Khaled would give you many pearls like this, if he married you. Will you not tell me?'

'Whom do you wish to kill?' Almasta asked, very suddenly. But Zehowah was unmoved.

'It may be that I have a private enemy,' she said. 'Perhaps there is one who disturbs me, against whom I plot in the night, but can find no way of ridding myself of him. A woman might give much to destroy such a one.'

'Khaled will kill your enemies. He loves you. He will kill all whom you hate.'

'You make progress. You speak our language better,' said Zehowah, laughing a little. 'You will soon be able to tell the Sultan that you love him, as well as I could myself.'

'But you do not love him,' Almasta answered boldly.

Zehowah bent her brows so that they met between her eyes as the grip of a bow. Then Khaled's heart leaped in his breast, for he saw that she was angry with the woman, and he supposed it was because she secretly loved him. But he held his breath lest even his breathing should betray him.

'The portion of fools is fire,' said Zehowah, not deigning to give any other answer. For she was a king's daughter and Almasta a bought slave, though Khaled had taken her in war.

'Be merciful!' exclaimed Almasta, in humble tones. 'I am your handmaid, and I speak Arabic badly.'

'You speak with exceeding clearness when it pleases you.'

'Indeed I cannot talk in your language, for it is not long since I came into Arabia.'

'We will have you taught, for we will give you a husband who will teach you with sticks. There is a certain hunchback, having one eye and marked with the smallpox, whose fists are as the feet of an old camel.

He will be a good husband for you and will teach you
the Arabic language, and your skin shall be dissolved
but your mind will be enlightened thereby.'

'Be merciful! I desire no husband.'

'It is good that a woman should marry, even though
the bridegroom be a hunchback. But if you will tell me
your secret I will give you a better husband and forgive
you.'

'There is no secret! I have killed no one!' cried
Almasta. 'Who has told you the lie?'

'And moreover,' continued Zehowah, not regarding
her protestations, 'there are other ways of learning
secrets, besides by kindness; such, for instance, as
sticks, and hot irons, and hunger and thirst in a prison
where there are reptiles and poisonous spiders, besides
many other things with which I have no doubt the
slaves of the palace are acquainted. It is better that
you should tell your secret and be happy.'

'There is no secret,' Almasta repeated, and she would
say nothing else, for she did not trust Zehowah and
feared a cruel death if she told the truth.

But Zehowah wearied of the contest at last, being by
no means sure that the woman had really done any
evil, and having no intention of using any violent means
such as she had suggested. For she was as just as she
was wise and would have no one suffer wrongly.
Khaled, indeed, cared little for the pain of others, hav-

ing seen much blood shed in war, and would have
caused Almasta to be tortured if Zehowah had desired
it. But she did not, preferring to wait and see whether
she could not entrap the slave into a confession.

Khaled now came out of his hiding-place into the
room and advanced towards Zehowah, who remained
sitting upon the carpet, while Almasta rose and made
a respectful salutation. But neither of the women
knew that he had been hidden in the niche. Zehowah
did not seem surprised, but Almasta's face was white
and her eyes were cast down, though indeed Khaled
wished that it had been otherwise. He was encouraged,
however, by what he had seen, for Zehowah had certainly
been angry with Almasta on his account, and he dis-
missed the latter that he might be alone with his wife.

'You are wise, Zehowah,' he said, 'and gifted with
much insight, but you will learn nothing from this
woman, though you talk with her a whole year. For
she suspects you and is guarded in her speech and
manner. I was standing by the doorway a long time.
You did not see me, but I heard all that you said.'

'Why did you hide yourself?' Zehowah asked, looking at him curiously.

'In order to listen,' he answered. 'And I heard
something and saw something which pleased me. For
when she said that you did not love me, you were
angry.'

'Did that please you? You are more easily pleased than I had thought. Shall I bear such things from a slave? How is it her business whether I love or not?'

'But you were angry,' Khaled repeated, vainly hoping that she would say more, yet not wishing to press her too far, lest she should say again that she did not love him.

She, however, said nothing in reply, but busied herself in taking his kefiyeh from his head and his sword from his side that he might be at ease. He rested against the cushions and drank of the cool drink she offered him.

'This woman, Almasta, is exceedingly beautiful,' he said at last. 'It would indeed be a pity that a slave of such value should go into the possession of another so that we could see her no more. It is best that you should keep her with you.'

Zehowah laughed a little, as she sat down beside him and began to play with her beads.

'This is what I have always said,' she answered. 'I will keep her with me.'

'It is better so,' said Khaled.

Then he remained silent in deep thought, having devised a new plan for gaining what he most desired. It seemed to him possible that Zehowah might be moved by jealousy, if by nothing else; for although he had sworn to her, and angrily, that he would never take

Almasta for his wife, and though nothing could really have prevailed upon him to make him do so, yet it would be easy for him to talk to the woman and speak to her of her beauty, and appear to take delight in her singing, which was more melodious than that of a Persian nightingale. Since she would be now permanently established in his harem, nothing would be easier than for him to spend many hours in the woman's society. Being a simple-minded man the plan seemed to him subtle, and he determined to put it into execution without delay. He knew also that Almasta had loved him since the first day when she had been brought before him in the palace at Haïl, and this would make it still more easy to rouse Zehowah's jealousy.

Though she had herself advised him to marry Almasta, he did not believe that she was greatly in earnest, and he felt assured that if the possibility were presented before her, in such a way as to appear imminent, she would be deceived by the appearance.

'It is better that she should remain here,' he said after a long time. 'For we cannot put her to death without evidence of her guilt, and if we are obstinate in wishing to give her a husband, we do not know how many husbands she may destroy before she is satisfied. She is beautiful, and will be an ornament in your kahwah. Indeed I do not know why I sent her away just now, when I came in. Let us call her back, that she may sing to us some of her own songs.'

Zehowah clapped her hands and Almasta immediately returned, for she had indeed been waiting outside the door, endeavouring to hear what was said, since she suspected that Khaled would speak of her and ask questions. She understood well enough, and often much better than she was willing to show, though she could as yet speak but few words of the Arabic language.

'Sit at my feet,' said Khaled, 'and sing to me the songs of your own people.'

Almasta took a musical instrument from the wall and sat down to sing. Her voice, indeed, was of enchanting sweetness, but as for the words of her songs, the seven wise men themselves could not have understood a syllable of them, seeing that they were neither Arabic nor Persian, nor even Greek. Nevertheless, Khaled made a pretence of being much pleased, resting his head against the cushions and closing his eyes as though the sound soothed him. As for Zehowah, she watched the woman with great curiosity, wondering whether it were possible that a creature so fair as Almasta could have done the evil deeds of which she was suspected, and planning how she might surprise her into a confession of guilt.

CHAPTER VII

NOT many days passed after this, before the women of the harem began to whisper among themselves in the passages and outer chambers.

'See,' they said, 'how our master favours this foreign woman, who is in all probability a devil from the Persian mountains. Every day he will have her to sing to him, and to bring him drink, and to sit at his feet. And he has given her several bracelets of gold and a large ruby. Surely it will be better for us to flatter her and show her reverence, for if not she will before long give us sticks to eat, and we shall mourn our folly.'

So they began to exhibit great respect for Almasta, giving her always the best seat amongst them and setting aside for her the best portions of the mutton, and the whitest of the rice, and the largest of the sweetmeats and the mellowest of the old sugar dates, so that Almasta fared sumptuously. But though she understood the reason why the women treated her so much more kindly than before, she was careful always to appear thankful and to speak softly to them, for she feared Zehowah, to whom they might speak of her, and who was very powerful with the Sultan. She was indeed secretly transported with joy, for she loved Khaled and she began to think that before long he would marry her. This was her only motive, also, for she was not otherwise ambitious, and though she afterwards did many evil deeds, she did them all out of love for him.

Though Khaled was by no means soft-hearted, he could not but pity her sometimes, seeing how she was deceived by his kindness, while he was only making a pretence of preferring her in order to gain Zehowah's love. Often he sat long with closed eyes while she sang to him or played softly upon the barbat, and he tried to fancy that the voice and the presence were Zehowah's. But her strange language disturbed him, for there were sounds in it like the hissing of serpents and like choking, which caused him to start suddenly just when her voice was sweetest. For the Georgian tongue is barbarous and not like any human speech under the sun, resembling by turns the inarticulate warbling of birds, and the croaking of ravens, and the noises made by an angry cat. Nevertheless, Khaled always made a pretence of being pleased, though he enjoined upon Almasta to learn to sing in Arabic.

'For Arabic,' he said to her, 'is the language of

K

paradise, and is spoken by all beings among the blessed, from Adam, our father, who waits for the resurrection in the first heaven, to the birds that fly among the branches of the tree Sedrat, near the throne of Allah, singing perpetually the verses of Al Koran. The black-eyed virgins reserved for the faithful, also speak only in Arabic.'

'Shall I be of the Hur al Oyun of whom you speak?' Almasta inquired.

'How is it possible that you should be of the black-eyed ones, when your eyes are blue?' Khaled asked, laughing. 'And besides, are you not an unbeliever?'

'I believe what you believe, and am learning your language. There is no Allah beside Allah.'

'And Mohammed is Allah's prophet.'

'And Mohammed is Allah's prophet,' Almasta repeated devoutly.

'Good. And the six articles of belief are also necessary.'

'Teach me,' said Almasta, laying the barbat upon the carpet and folding her hands.

'You must believe first in Allah, and secondly in all the angels. Thirdly you must believe in Al Koran, fourthly in the prophets of Allah, fifthly in the resurrection of the dead and the last judgment, and lastly that your destiny is about your neck so that you cannot escape it.'

'I believe in everything,' said Almasta, who understood nothing of these sacred matters. 'Shall I now
be one of the Hur al Oyun?'

'But you have blue eyes.'

'When I know that I am dying, I will paint them
black,' said Almasta, laughing sweetly.

'The angels Monkar and Nakir will discover your
deception,' said Khaled. 'When you are dead and
buried, these two angels, who are black, will enter
your tomb. They are of extremely terrible appearance.
Then they will make you sit upright in the grave and
will examine you first as to your belief and then as
to your deeds. You will then not be able to tell lies.
If you truly believe and have done good, your soul
will then be breathed out of your lips and will float
in a state of rest over your grave until the last judgment. But if not, the black angels will beat your
head with iron maces, and tear your soul from your
body with a torment greater than that caused by
tearing the flesh from the bones.'

'I believe in everything,' Almasta said again, supposing that her assent would please him.

'You find it an easy matter to believe what I tell
you,' he said, for he could see that she would have
received any other faith as readily. 'But it is not
easy for a woman to enter paradise, and since it is
your destiny to have blue eyes, they will not become

black.　The Hur al Oyun, however, are not mortal
women and no mortal woman can ever be one of
them, since they are especially prepared for the faithful.　But a man's wives may enter paradise with him,
in a glorified beauty which may not be inferior to that
of the black-eyed ones.　If, for instance, Abdul Kerim
had lived and been your husband, you might, by faith
and good works, have entered heaven with him as one
of his wives.'

Almasta looked long at Khaled, trying to see
whether he still suspected her, and indeed he found
it very hard to do so, for her look was clear and
innocent as that of a young dove that is fed by a
familiar hand.

'I would like to enter paradise with you,' said
Almasta, with an appearance of timidity.　'Is it not
possible?'

'It may be possible.　But I doubt it,' Khaled
answered, with gravity.

In those days, while Khaled thus spent many
hours with Almasta, Zehowah often remained for a
long time in another part of the harem, either surrounded by her women, or sitting alone upon the
balcony over the court, absorbed in watching the
people who came and went.　The slaves were surprised to see that Khaled seemed to prefer the society
of the Georgian to that of his wife, but they dared say

nothing to Zehowah and contented themselves with watching her face and endeavouring to find out whether she were displeased at what was happening, or really indifferent as she appeared to be.

Almasta herself was distrustful, supposing that Khaled and Zehowah were in league together to entrap her into a self-accusation, and though her heart was transported with happiness while she was with Khaled, yet she did not forget to be cautious whenever any reference was made to Abdul Kerim's death. She also took the long needle out of her hair and hid it carefully in a corner, in a crevice between the pavement and the wall, lest it should at any time fall from its place and bring suspicion upon her.

Khaled watched Zehowah as narrowly as the women did, to see whether any signs of jealousy showed themselves in her face, and sometimes they talked together of Almasta.

'It is strange,' said Khaled, 'that Allah, being all powerful, should have provided matter for dissension on earth by creating one woman more beautiful than another, the one with blue eyes, the other with black, the one with red hair and the other with hair needing henna to brighten it. Are not all women the children of one mother?'

'And are not all men her sons also?' asked Zehowah. 'It is strange that Allah, being all powerful, should have provided matter for sorrow by creating one man with a spirit easily satisfied, and the other with a soul tormented by discontent.'

Khaled looked fixedly at his wife, and bent his brows. But in secret he was glad, for he supposed that she was beginning to be jealous. However, he made a pretence of being displeased.

'Is man a rock that he should never change?' he asked. 'Or has he but one eye with which to see but one kind of beauty?   Have I not two hands, two feet, two ears, two nostrils and two eyes?'

'That is true,' Zehowah answered. 'But a man has only one heart with which to love, one voice with which to speak kind words, and one mouth with which to kiss the woman he has chosen.   And if a man had two souls, they would rend him so that he would be mad.'

At this Khaled laughed a little and would gladly have shown Zehowah that she was right. But he feared to be treated with indifference, if he yielded to her argument so soon, and he held his peace.

'Nevertheless,' Zehowah continued, after a time, 'you are right and so am I.   You said, indeed, not many days ago that your two hands should wither at the wrists if you took another wife, yet I advised you to do so; and now it is clear from what you say that you wish to marry Almasta.   I am your handmaiden. Take her, therefore, and be contented, for she loves you.'

But now Khaled was much disturbed as to what he should answer, for he had hoped that Zehowah would break out into jealous anger. He could not accept her advice, because of his oath and still more because of his love for her; yet he could not send away Almasta, since by so doing he would be giving over his last hope of obtaining Zehowah's love by rousing her jealousy.

'Take her,' Zehowah repeated. 'The palace is wide and spacious. There is room for us both, and for two others also, if need be, according to divine law. Take her, and let there be contentment. Have you not said that she is more beautiful than I?'

'No,' answered Khaled, 'I have not said so.'

'You have thought it, which is much the same, for you said that her hair was red but that mine needed henna to brighten it. Marry her therefore, this very day. Send for the Kadi, and order a feast, and let it be done quickly.'

'Is it nothing to you, whether I take her or not?' Khaled asked, seeking desperately for something to say.

'Is it for me to set myself up against the holy law? Or did any one exact from you a promise that you would not take another wife? And if you rashly promised anything of your own free will, the promise is not binding seeing that there is no authority for

it in Al Koran, and that no one desires you to keep
it—neither I, nor Almasta.'

Zehowah laughed at her own speech, and Khaled was
too much disturbed to notice that the laugh was rather
of scorn than of mirth.

'How shall I take a woman who is perhaps a
murderess?' he asked. 'Shall I take her who was
perhaps the cause of your revered father's death?
May Allah give him peace! Surely, the very thought
is terrible to me, and I will not do it.'

'Will you convict her without witnesses? And
where is your witness? Did not the physician
explain the reason of the death, and did he suspect
that there was anything unnatural about it? But
if you still think that she destroyed my father and
Abdul Kerim—peace on them both—why do you
make her sit all day long at your feet and sing to
you in her barbarous language, which resembles the
barking of jackals? And why do you command
her to bring you drink and fan you when it is
hot, and you sleep in the afternoon? This shows
a forgiving and trustful disposition.'

'This is an unanswerable argument,' thought Khaled,
being very much perplexed. 'Can I answer that I do
all this in order to see whether Zehowah is jealous?
She would certainly laugh to herself and say in her
heart that she has married a fool.'

So he said nothing, but bent his brows again, and endeavoured to seem angry. But Zehowah took no notice of his face and continued to urge him to marry Almasta.

'Have you ever seen such a woman?' she asked. 'Have you ever seen such eyes? Are they not like twin heavens of a deep blue, each having a shining sun in the midst? Is not her hair like seventy thousand pieces of gold poured out upon the carpet from a height? Her nose is a straight piece of pure ivory. Her lips are redder than pomegranates when they are ripe, and her cheeks are as smooth as silk. Moreover she is as white as milk, freshly taken from the camel, whereas my hands are of the colour of blanket-bread before it is baked.'

'Your hands are much smaller than hers,' said Khaled, who could not suffer Zehowah to discredit her own beauty.

'I do not know,' she answered, looking at her fingers. 'But they are less white. And Almasta is far more beautiful than I. You yourself said so.'

'I never said so,' Khaled replied, more and more perplexed. 'There are two kinds of beauty. That is what I said. Allah has willed it. Almasta is a slave, and her hands are large. It is a pity, for she is like a mare that has many good points, but whose hoofs are overgrown through too much idleness in the stable. I

say that there are two kinds of beauty. Yours is that
of the free woman of a pure and beautiful race; hers
is that of the slave accidentally born beautiful.'

Zehowah gathered up her three long black tresses
and laid them across her knees as she sat. Then she
shook off her golden bracelets, one after the other, to the
number of a score and heaped them upon the hair.

'Which do you like best?' she asked. 'The black
or the gold? The day or the night? Here you see
them together and can judge fairly between them.'

Khaled sought for a crafty answer and made a pretence of pondering the matter deeply.

'After the night,' he said at last, 'the day is very
bright and glorious. But when we have looked on it
long, only the night can bring rest and peace.'

He was pleased with himself when he had made
this answer, supposing that Zehowah would find
nothing to say. But he had only laid a new trap
for himself.

'That is quite true,' she answered, laughing. 'That
is also the reason why Allah made the day and the
night to follow each other in succession, lest men
should grow weary of eternal light or eternal darkness. For the same reason also, since you have a
wife whose hair is black, I counsel you to take a
red-haired one. In this way you will obtain that
variety which the taste of man craves.'

'If I follow your advice, you will regret it,' said Khaled.

'You think I shall be jealous, but you are mistaken. I am what I am. Can another woman make me more or less beautiful? Moreover, I shall always be first in the palace, though you take three other wives. The others will rise up when you come in, but I shall remain sitting. I shall always be the first wife.'

'Undoubtedly, that is your right,' Khaled replied. 'Do you suppose that I wish to put any woman in your place?'

Then Zehowah laughed, and laid her hand upon Khaled's arm.

'How foolish men are!' she exclaimed. 'Do you think you can deceive me? Do you imagine, because I have answered you and talked with you to-day, and listened to your arguments, that I do not understand your heart? Oh, Khaled, this is true which you often say of yourself, that your wit is in your arm. If I were a warrior and stood before you with a sword in my hand, you could argue better, for you would cut off my head, and the argument would end suddenly. But Allah has not made you subtle, and words in your mouth are of no more avail than a sword would be in mine, for you entangle yourself in your own language, as I should wound myself if I tried to handle a weapon.'

At this Khaled was much disconcerted, and he stroked his beard thoughtfully, looking away so as not to meet her eyes.

'I do not know what you mean,' he said, at last. You certainly imagine something which has no existence.'

'I imagine nothing, for I have seen the truth, ever since the first day when you desired to be alone with Almasta. You are only foolishly trying to make me jealous of her, in order that I may love you better.'

When Khaled saw that she understood him, he was without any defence, for he had built a wall of sand for himself, like a child playing in the desert, which the first breath of wind causes to crumble, and the second blast leaves no trace of it behind.

'And am I foolish, because I have done this thing?' he cried, not attempting to deny the truth. 'Am I a fool because I desire your love? But it is folly to speak of it, for you will reproach me and say that I am discontented, and will offer me another woman for my wife. Go. Leave me alone. If you do not love me, the sight of you is as vinegar poured into a fresh wound, and as salt rubbed into eyes that are sore with the sand. Go. Why do you stay? Do you not believe me? Do you wish me to kill you that I may have peace from you? It is a pity that you did not marry one of the hundred suitors who came before me, for you certainly loved one of them, since you cannot love me. You doubtless loved the Indian prince. Would you have him back? I can give you his bones, for I slew him with my own hands and buried him in the Red Desert, where his soul is sitting upon a heap of sand, waiting for the day of resurrection.'

Then Zehowah was greatly astonished, for neither she nor any one else had ever known what had been the end of that suitor, and after waiting a long time, his people who had been with him had departed sorrowing to their own country, and she had heard no more of them.

'What is this?' she asked in amazement. 'Why did you kill him? And how could you have done this thing unseen, since he was guarded by many attendants?'

'I took him out of the palace in the night, when all were asleep, and then I killed him,' said Khaled, and Zehowah could get no other answer, for he would not confess that he had been one of the genii, lest she should not believe the truth, or else, believing, should be afraid of him in the future.

'I will give you his bones,' he said, 'if you desire them, for I know where they are, and you certainly loved him, and are still mourning for him. If he could be alive, I would kill him again.'

'I never loved him,' Zehowah answered, at last.

'How was it possible? But I would perhaps have married him, hoping to convert all his people to the true faith.'

'As you have married me in the hope, or the assurance, of giving your people a just king.'

'You are angry, Khaled. And, indeed, I could be angry, too, but with myself and not with you, as you are with me, though it be for the same reason. For I begin to see and understand why you are discontented, and indeed I will do what I can to satisfy you.'

'You must love me, as I love you, if you would save me from destruction,' said Khaled.

Though Zehowah could not comprehend the meaning of the words, she saw by his face that he was terribly moved, and she herself began to be more sorry for him.

'Indeed, Khaled,' she said, 'I will try to love you from this hour. But it is a hard thing, because you cannot explain it, and it is not easy to learn what cannot be explained. Do you think that all women love their husbands in this way you mean? Am I unlike all the rest?'

Khaled took her hand and held it, and looked into her eyes.

'Love is the first mystery of the world,' he said. 'Death is the second. Between the two there is nothing but a weariness darkened with shadows and thick with mists. What is gold? A cinder that glows in the darkness for a moment and falls away to a cold ash in our hand when we have taken it. But love is a treasure which remains. What is renown? A cry uttered in the bazar by men whose minds are subject to change as their bodies are to death. But the voice of love is heard in paradise, singing beside the fountains Tasnim and Salsahil. What is power? A net with which to draw wealth and fame from the waters of life? To what end? We must die. Or is power a sword to kill our enemies? If their time is come they will die without the sword. Or is it a stick to purify the hides of fools? The fool will die also, like his master, and both will be forgotten. But they who love shall enter the seventh heaven together, according to the promise of Allah. Death is stronger than man or woman, but love is stronger than death, and all else is but a vision seen in the desert, having no reality.'

'I will try to understand it, for I see that you are very unhappy,' said Zehowah.

She was silent after this, for Khaled's words were earnest and sank into her soul. Yet the more she tried to imagine what the passion in him could be like, the less she was able to understand it, for some of Khaled's actions had been foolish, but she supposed that there must have been some wisdom in them, having its foundation in the nature of love.

'What he says is true,' she thought. 'I married him in order to give my people a just and brave king, and he is both brave and just. And I am certainly a good wife, for I should be dissolved in shame if another man were to see my face, and moreover I am careful of his wants, and I take his kefiyeh from his head with my own hands, and smooth the cushions for him and bring him food and drink when he desires it. Or have I withheld from him any of the treasures of the palace, or stood in the way of his taking another wife? Until to-day, I thought indeed that this talk of love meant but little, and that he spoke of it because he desired an excuse for marrying Almasta who loves him. But when I said at a venture that he wished to make me jealous, he confessed the truth. Now all the tales of love told by the old women are of young persons who have seen each other from a distance, but are hindered from marrying. And we are already married. Surely, it is very hard to understand.'

After this Khaled never called Almasta to sit at his feet and sing to him, as he had done before, and Zehowah was constantly with him in her stead. At first Almasta supposed that Khaled only made a pretence of disregarding her, out of respect for his wife,

but she soon perceived that he was indifferent and no
longer noticed her. She then grew fierce and jealous,
and her voice was not heard singing in the harem;
but she went and took her needle again from the
crevice in the pavement and hid it in her hair, and
though Zehowah often called her, when Khaled was
not in the house, she made as though she understood
even less of the Arabic language than before and sat
stupidly on the carpet, gazing at her hands. Zehowah
wearied of her silence, for she understood the reason
of it well enough.

'I am tired of this woman,' she said to Khaled.
'Do you think I am jealous of her now?'

Khaled smiled a little, but said nothing, only
shaking his head.

'I am tired of her,' Zehowah repeated. 'She sits
before me like a sack of barley in a grainseller's shop,
neither moving nor speaking.'

'She is yours,' Khaled answered. 'Send her away.
Or we will give her in marriage to one of the sheikhs
who will take her away to the desert. In this way
she will not be able even to visit you except when her
husband comes into the city.'

But they decided nothing at that time. Some
days later Khaled was sitting alone upon a balcony,
Zehowah having gone to the bath, when Almasta came
suddenly before him and threw herself at his feet,

beating her forehead and tearing her hair, though not
indeed in a way to injure it.

'What have I done?' she cried. 'Why is my
lord displeased?'

Khaled looked at her in surprise, but answered
nothing at first.

'Why are my lord's eyes like frozen pools by the
Kura, and why is his forehead like Kasbek in a mist?'

Khaled laughed a little at her words.

'Kasbek is far from Riad,' he answered, 'and the
waters of the Kura do not irrigate the Red Desert. I
am not displeased. On the contrary, I will give you
a husband and a sufficient dowry. Go in peace.'

But Almasta remained where she was, weeping and
beating her forehead.

'Let me stay!' she cried. 'Let me stay, for I love
you. I will eat the dust under your feet. Only let
me stay.'

'I think not,' Khaled answered. 'You weary
Zehowah with your silence and your sullenness.'

'Let me stay!' she repeated, over and over again.

She was not making any pretence of grief, for the
tears ran down abundantly and stained the red leather
of Khaled's shoes. Though he was hard-hearted he
was not altogether cruel, for a man who loves one
woman greatly is somewhat softened towards all such
as do not stand immediately in his way.

'It is true,' he thought, 'that I have given this woman some occasion of hope, for I have treated her kindly during many days, and she has probably supposed that I would marry her. For she is less keen-sighted than Zehowah, and moreover she loves me.'

'Do not drive me out!' cried Almasta. 'For I shall die if I cannot see your face. What have I done?'

'You have indeed done nothing worthy of death, for I cannot prove that you killed Abdul Kerim. I will therefore give you a good husband and you shall be happy.'

But Almasta would not go away, and embracing his knees she looked up into his face, imploring him to let her remain. Khaled could not but see that she was beautiful, for the mid-day light fell upon her white face and her red lips, and made shadows in her hair of the colour of mellow dates, and reflections as bright as gold when the burnisher is still in the goldsmith's hand. Though he cared nothing for Almasta and little for her sorrow, his eye was pleased and he smiled.

Then he looked up and saw Zehowah standing before him, just as she had come from the bath, wrapped in loose garments of silk and gold. He gazed at her attentively for there was a distant gleam of light in her eyes and her cheeks were warm, though she stood in the shadow, so that he thought she had never been more beautiful, and he did not care to look at Almasta's face again.

'Why is Almasta lamenting in this way?' Zehowah asked.

'She desires to stay in the palace,' Khaled answered; 'but I have told her that she shall be married, and yet she wishes to stay.'

'Let her be married quickly, then. Is she a free woman, that she should resist, or is she rich that she should refuse alms? Let her be married.'

'There is a certain young man, cousin to Abdul Kerim, a Bedouin of pure descent. Let him take her, if he will, and let the marriage be celebrated to-morrow.'

But Almasta shook her head, and her tears never ceased from flowing.

'You will marry him,' said Khaled. 'And if any harm comes to him, I will cause you to be put to death before the second call to prayer on the following morning.'

When Almasta heard this, her tears were suddenly dried and her lips closed tightly. She rose from the floor and retired to a distance within the room.

On that day Khaled sent for the young man of whom he had spoken, whose name was Abdullah ibn Mohammed el Herir, and offered him Almasta for a wife. And he accepted her joyfully, for he had heard of her wonderful beauty, and was moreover much gratified by being given a woman whom the former Sultan would probably have married if he had lived. Khaled also gave him a grey mare as a wedding gift, and a handsome garment.

The marriage was therefore celebrated in the customary manner, and no harm came to Abdullah. But as the autumn had now set in, he soon afterwards left the city, taking Almasta with him, to live in tents, after the manner of the Bedouins.

CHAPTER VIII

ABDULLAH IBN MOHAMMED, though a young man, was
now the sheikh of a considerable tribe which had
frequently done good service to the late Sultan,
Zehowah's father, and which had also borne a promi-
nent part in the recent war. Abdul Kerim, whom
Almasta had murdered, had been the sheikh during
his lifetime, and if the claims of birth had been justly
considered, his son, though a mere boy, should have
succeeded him. But Abdullah had found it easy to
usurp the chief place, and in the council which was
held after Abdul Kerim's death he was chosen by
acclamation. It chanced, too, that he was not married at the time when he took Almasta, for of two
wives the one had died of a fever during the summer,
and he had divorced the other on account of her
unbearable temper, having been deceived in respect of
this by her parents, who had assured him that she was
as gentle as a dove and as submissive as a lamb. But
she had turned out to be as quarrelsome as a wasp
and as unmanageable as an untrained hawk, so he

divorced her, and the more readily because she was
not beautiful and her dower had been insignificant.
Almasta therefore found that she was her husband's
only wife.

She would certainly have killed him, as she had
killed Abdul Kerim, and, indeed, the late Sultan, in
the hope of being taken back into the palace, but she
was prevented by the fear of death, for she had seen
that Khaled's threat was not empty and would be
executed if harm came to Abdullah after his marriage.
She accordingly set herself to please him, and first of
all she learned to speak the Arabic language, in order
that she might sing to him in his own tongue and tell
him tales of distant countries, which she had learned
in her own home.

Abdullah passed the months of autumn and the
early winter in the desert, moving about from place to
place, as is the custom of the Bedouins, it being his
intention to reach a northerly point of Ajman in the
spring, in order to fall upon the Persian pilgrims and
extort a ransom before they entered the territory of
Nejed. For it would not be lawful to attack them
after that, since there was a treaty with the Emir of
Basrah, allowing the pilgrims a safe and free passage
towards Mecca, for which the Emir paid yearly a sum
of money to the Sultan of Nejed.

But Almasta knew nothing of this, for she was

wholly ignorant of the desert; and moreover Abdullah was a cautious man, who held that whatsoever is to be kept secret must not be uttered aloud, though there be no one within three days' journey to hear it.

Abdullah treated her with great consideration, not obliging her to weary herself overmuch with cooking and other work of the tents. For he rejoiced in her beauty and in the sweetness of her voice, and his chief delight was to sit in the door of the tent at night, chewing frankincense, while Almasta sat within, close behind him, and told him tales of her own country, or of the life in the palace of Riad. The latter indeed was as strange to him as the former, and much more interesting.

Now one evening they were alone together in this manner, and it was not yet very cold. But the stars shone brightly as though there would be a frost before morning, and the other tents were all closed and no one was near the coals which remained from the fire after baking the blanket-bread. One might hear the chewing of the camels in the dark and the tramping of a mare that moved slowly about, her hind feet being chained together.

'Tell me more of the palace at Riad,' said Abdullah. 'For your Kura, and your snow-covered Kasbek, and your Tiflis with its warm springs and gardens, I shall never see. But I have seen the courts of the

palace from my youth, and the Sultan's kahwah, and
the latticed windows of the harem, from which you
say that you saw me and loved me in the last days of
summer.'

Almasta had said this to please him, though it
was not true. For she knew that men easily believe
what flatters them, as women believe that what they
desire must come to pass.

'The palace is a wonderful palace,' said Almasta,
'and I will tell you of the treasures which are in it.'

'That is what I wish to hear,' answered Abdullah,
putting a piece of frankincense into his mouth and
beginning to chew it.   'Tell me of the treasures, for
it is said that they are great and of extraordinary
value.'

'The value of them cannot be calculated, O Abdullah, for if you had seventy thousand hands and
on each hand seventy thousand fingers you could not
count upon your fingers in a whole lifetime the gold
sherifs and sequins and tomans which are hidden
away there in bags.   Beneath the court of strangers
there is a great chamber built of stone in which the
sacks of gold are kept, and they are piled up to the
roof of the vault on all sides and in the middle,
leaving only narrow passages between.'

'If it is all gold, what is the use of the passages?
asked Abdullah.

'I do not know, but they are there, and there is another room filled with silver in the same manner. There are also secret places underground in which jewels are kept in chests, rubies and pearls and Indian diamonds and emeralds, in such quantities that they would suffice to make necklaces of a thousand rows each for each of the mountains in my country. And we have many mountains, great ones, not such as the little hills you have seen, but several days' journey in height. For we say that when the Lord made the earth it was at first unsteady, and He set our mountains upon it, in the middle, to make it firm, and it has never moved since.'

'I do not believe this,' said Abdullah. 'Tell me more about the jewels in Riad.'

'There is no end of them. They are like the grains of sand in the desert, and no one of them is worth less than a thousand gold sherifs. I do not even know the names of the different kinds, but there are turquoises without number, of the Maidan, and all good, so that you may write upon them with a piece of gold as with a pen; and there are red stones as large as a dove's egg, red and fiery as the wine of Kachetia, and others, blue as the sky in winter, and yellow ones, and some with leaves of gold in them, like morsels of treng floating in the juice. But besides the gold and silver and precious stones there are thousands of rich garments which are kept in chests of fragrant wood, in upper chambers, abas woven of gold and silk and linen, and vests embroidered with pearls, and shoes of which even the soles appear to be of gold. And there are great pieces of stuff, Indian silk, and Persian velvet, and even satin from Stamboul, woven by unbelievers with the help of devils. Then too, in the palace of Riad, there are stored great quantities of precious weapons, most of them made in Syria, with many swords of Shām, which you say are the best, though I do not understand the matter, each having an inscription in letters of gold upon the blade, and the hilt most cunningly chiselled in the same metal, or carved out of ivory.'

'I saw the treasure of Haïl when we took it away after the war, and most of it was distributed among us, but there was nothing like this,' said Abdullah.

'The treasure of Haïl is to the treasure of Riad, as a small black fly walking upon the face of the sun,' answered Almasta. 'And yet there was wealth there also, and there was much which you never saw. For that Khaled, who is now Sultan, is crafty and avaricious, and he loaded many camels secretly by night, being helped by black slaves, all of whom he slew afterwards with his own hand lest they should tell the tale, and he then called camel-drivers and sent them away with the beasts to Riad. And he said to them:

" These are certain loads of fine wheat and of mellow dates, for the Sultan's table, such as cannot be found in Riad." But he sent a letter to his father-in-law, who caused all the packs to be taken immediately to one of the secret chambers, where he and his daughter Zehowah took out the jewels and stored them with their own. And as for me, I believe that Khaled made an end of the Sultan himself by means of poison in Dereyiyah, for he rode away suddenly after they had met, as though his conscience smote him.'

' What is this evil tale which you are telling me ?' cried Abdullah. ' Surely, it is a lie, for Khaled is a brave man who gives every one his due and deceives no one. And he is by no means subtle, for I have heard him in council, and he generally said only, " Smite," but sometimes he said " Strike," and that was all his eloquence. But whether he said the one or the other, he was generally the first to follow his own advice which, indeed, by the merciful dispensation of Allah, procured us the victory. But what is this tale which you have invented ? '

' And who is this Khaled whom you praise ? ' asked Almasta. ' And how can you know his crafti-ness as I know it, who have lived in the palace and braided his wife's hair, and brought him drink when he was thirsty ? Is he a man of your tribe whose descent you can count upon your fingers, from him to his grandfather and to Ishmael and Abraham? Or is he a man of a tribe known to you, and whose generations you also know? Has any man called him Khaled ibn Mohammed, or Khaled ibn Abdullah? Or has he ever spoken of his father, who is probably now drinking boiling water, and the black angels are pounding his head with iron maces. Yet he says that he came from the desert. Then you, who are of the desert, do not know the desert, for you do not know whence he is. But there are those who do know, and he fears them, lest they should tell the truth and destroy him.'

'These are idle tales,' said Abdullah. 'Is it probable that the Sultan would have bestowed his daughter and all the treasures you have described upon such a man without having made inquiries concerning his family. And if the Sultan said nothing to us about it, and if Khaled holds his peace, they have doubtless their reasons. For it may be that there is a blood feud between the people of Khaled and some great person in Riad, so that he would be in danger of his life if he revealed his father's name. Allah knows. It is not our business.'

'O Abdullah, you are simple, and you believe all things!' cried Almasta. 'But I heard of him in Basrah.'

'What did you hear in Basrah? And how could you have heard of him there?'

'I was in the Emir's harem, being kept there to rest from the journey after they had brought me from the north. And there I heard of Khaled, for the women talked of him, having been told tales about him by a merchant who was admitted to the palace.'

'Now this is great folly,' answered Abdullah. 'For Khaled came suddenly to Riad, and was married immediately to Zehowah, and on the next day he went out with us against Haïl, which we took from the Shammar in three weeks' time from the day of our marching. Moreover we found you there in the palace. How then could news of Khaled have reached Basrah before you left that place?'

'I had come to Haïl but the day before you attacked the city,' said Almasta. 'But did I say that I had heard of him as already married to Zehowah?'

For she saw that she had run the risk of being found out in a lie, and she made haste to defend herself.

'What did you hear of him?' asked Abdullah.

'He was a notable fellow and a robber,' answered Almasta. 'For he is a Persian, and a Shiyah, who offers prayers to Ali in secret. But because he had done many outrageous deeds, a great price was set upon his head throughout Persia, so he fled into Arabia and by his boldness and craft he married Zehowah. And now he has made a secret covenant to deliver over the kingdom of Nejed to the Persians.'

Then Abdullah laughed aloud.

'Who shall deliver over the Bedouin to a white-faced people, who live on boiled chestnuts and ride astride of a camel? And when a man has got a kingdom, why should he give it up to any one, except under force?'

'There is a reason for this, too,' Almasta answered unabashed. 'For the King of the Persians, whom they call the Padeshah, has an only daughter, of great beauty, and Khaled is to receive her in marriage as the price of Nejed. Then he will by treachery destroy the Padeshah's sons and will inherit Persia also, as he has inherited Nejed; and after that he will make war upon the Romans in Stamboul and will become the master of the whole world.'

'This is a strange tale, and seems full of madness,' said Abdullah. 'I do not believe it. Tell me rather a story of your own country, and afterwards we will sleep, for to-morrow we will leave this place.'

'I will tell you a wonderful history, which is quite true,' answered Almasta. 'Take this fresh piece of frankincense which I have prepared for you, and put it into your mouth, for you will then not interrupt me with questions while I am speaking.'

So Abdullah took the savoury gum and chewed it, and Almasta told him the tale which here follows.

'There is in the north, beyond Persia, a great and

prosperous kingdom, lying between two seas, and resembling paradise for its wonderful beauty. All the hills are covered with trees of every description in which innumerable birds make their nests, all of a beautiful plumage and good for man to eat. And in these forests there are also great herds of animals, whose name I do not know in Arabic, having branching horns and kindred to the little beast which you call the cow of the desert, but far better to eat and as large as full-grown camels. A man who is hungry need only shoot an arrow at a venture, for the birds and animals are so numerous that he will certainly hit something. This kingdom is watered everywhere by rivers and streams abounding in fish, all good to eat and easily caught, and all the valleys are filled with vineyards of black and white grapes. But the people of this country are chiefly Christians. May Allah send them enlightenment! Now the King was an old man, who delighted in feasting and cared little for the affairs of the nation, preferring a lute to a sword, and a wine-cup to a shield, and the feet of dancing girls to the hoofs of war horses. He had no son to go out to war for him, but only one beautiful daughter.'

'Like the Sultan of our country who died,' said Abdullah.

'Very much. There were also other points of resemblance. Now there was a certain Tartar in the kingdom of Samarkand, called Ismaïl, who was a robber and had destroyed many caravans on the march, and had broken into many houses both in Samarkand and Tashkent, a notable evildoer. But having one day stolen a fleet mare from the Sultan's stables, the soldiers pursued him, and in order to escape impalement he fled. No one could catch him because the mare he had stolen was the fleetest in Great Tartary. So he rode westward through many countries, and by the shores of the inland sea, until he came to the kingdom which I have described. There he hid himself in the forest for some time and waylaid travellers, making them tell him all that they knew of the kingdom, and afterwards killing them. But when he had obtained all that he wanted, both rich garments and splendid weapons, and the necessary information, he left the forest and rode into the capital city. Then he went to the King and desired of him a private audience, which was granted. He said that he was the son of a powerful Christian prince, and had been taken captive by the Tartars, but had escaped, and he offered to make all Tartary subject to the King, if only he might marry his daughter. And whether by magic, or by eloquence, he succeeded, for the King was old and feeble-minded. But soon after the wedding, he poisoned his father-in-law and became king in his place, though there were many in the land who had a better right, being closely connected with the royal blood.'

'This is the story of Khaled,' said Abdullah. 'I know the truth. Why do you weary me, trying to deceive me, and calling him a robber? But it is true that in Nejed there are men of good descent who have a better right to sit on the throne.'

'Hear what followed,' answered Almasta. 'This man Ismaïl afterwards took captive a woman of the Tartars, who knew who he was, though he supposed her ignorant. And he gave her in marriage to the youngest and bravest of his captains, a man to whom Allah had vouchsafed the tongue of eloquence, and the teeth of strength, and the lips of discretion to close together and hide both at the proper season. The woman told her husband who Ismaïl was, and instructed him concerning the palace, its passages and secret places, and the treasures that were hidden there. And she told him also that Ismaïl had made a covenant with the Sultan of his own country, which would bring destruction upon the nation he now ruled. For she loved her husband on account of his youth and beauty, and she had embraced his faith and was ready to die for him.'

'The husband's name was Abdullah,' said Abdullah. 'And he also loved his wife, who surpassed other women in beauty, as a bay mare surpasses pigs.'

'He afterwards loved her still better,' answered Almasta, 'for though he was only chief over four hundred tents, she gave him a kingdom. Hear what followed. But I will call him Abdullah if you please, though his name was Mskhet.'

'Allah is merciful! There are no such names in Arabia. This one is like the breaking of earthen vessels upon stones. Call him Abdullah.'

'Abdullah therefore went to the wisest and most discreet of his kindred, and spoke to them of the great treasures which were hidden in the palace, and he pointed out to their obscured sight that all this wealth had been got by them and their fathers in war, and had been taken in tithes from the people, and was now in the possession of Ismaïl. And they talked among themselves and saw that this was indeed true. And at another time, he told them that Ismaïl was not really of their religion, but a hypocrite. And again a third time he told them the whole truth, so that their hearts burned when they knew that their King was but a robber who had been condemned to death. Though they were discreet men, the story was in some way told abroad among the soldiers, doubtless by the intervention of angels, so that all the people knew it, and were angry against Ismaïl and ready to break out against him so soon as a man could be found to lead them.

'But,' said Abdullah, 'this Ismaïl doubtless had a strong guard of soldiers about him, and had given gifts to his captains, and shown honour to them, so that they were attached to him.'

'Undoubtedly,' replied Almasta, 'and but for his wife, Abdullah could not have succeeded. She advised him to go to his discreet kindred and friends and say to them, " See, if you will afterwards support me, I will go alone into the palace and will get the better of this Ismaïl, when he is asleep, and I will so do that the soldiers shall not oppose me. And afterwards, you will all enter together and the treasure shall be divided. But we will throw some of it to the people, lest they be disappointed." And so he did. For his wife knew the secret entrances to the palace and took him in with her by night, disguised as a woman. And they went together silently into the harem, and slew Ismaïl and bound his wife, and took the keys of the treasure chambers from under the pillow. After this they took from the gold as many bags as there were soldiers, and waked each man, giving him a sack of sherifs, and bidding him take as much more as he could find, for the King was dead. Then Abdullah's friends were admitted and they divided the treasure, and went abroad before it was day, calling upon the people that Ismaïl was dead and that a man of their own nation was King in his place, and scattering handfuls of gold into

every house as they passed. And, behold, before the
second call to prayer, Abdullah was King, and all the
people came and did homage to him. And Abdullah
himself was astonished when he saw how easy it had
been, and loved his wife even better than before.'

So Almasta finished her tale and there was silence
for a time, while Abdullah sat still and gazed at the
closed tents in the starlight, and listened to the distant
chewing of the camels.

'Give me some water,' he said at last. 'I am very
thirsty.'

She brought him drink from the skin, and soon
afterwards he lay down to rest. But they said nothing
more to each other that night of the story which Almasta had told.

On the following day they journeyed fully eleven
hours, to a place where there was much water, and
in the evening, when the camels were chewing, and
all the Bedouins had eaten and were resting in
their tents, Abdullah sat again in his accustomed
place.

'Almasta, light of my darkness,' he said, 'I would
gladly hear again something of the tale you told me
last night, for I have not remembered it well, being
overburdened with the cares of my people and the
direction of the march. Surely you said that when
the woman and her husband had killed Ismaïl they

took the keys of the treasure chambers from under his pillow.   Is it not so ? '

'They did so, Abdullah.'

'And they immediately went and took the gold and gave it to the guards ?   But I have forgotten, for it is a matter of little importance, being but a tale.'

'That is what they did,' answered Almasta.

'But surely this is a fable.   How could the woman know the way to the treasure chambers and find it in the dark ?   For you said also that these secret places were underground and therefore a great way from the harem.'

'I did not say that, Abdullah, for the secret places underground are those in Riad, which I described to you before I began the other story.'

'This may be true, for I am very forgetful.   But I daresay that the treasures in the city you described were also hidden in similar places.'

'Since you speak of this, I remember that it was so.   The glorious light of your intelligence penetrates the darkness of my memory and makes it clear.   The places were exactly similar.'

'How then could the woman, who only knew the harem, find her way in the dark, and lead her husband, to a part of the palace which she had never visited ? This is a hard thing.'

'It was not hard for her.   She had seen Ismaïl

open with his key a door in his sleeping chamber, and
he had gone in and after some time had returned
bearing sacks of gold pieces.   Was this a hard thing?
Or does a wise man make two doors to his treasure-
house, the one for himself and the other for thieves?
The one leading to his own chamber, for his own use,
and the other opening upon the highway for the con-
venience of robbers?   It is possible, but I think not.
Ismaïl had but one door.   He was not an Egyptian
jackass.'

'This is reasonable,' said Abdullah.   'And I am
now satisfied.   But my imagination was not at rest, for
the story is a good one and deserves to be well told.'

After this Abdullah wandered for a long time with
the Bedouins who accompanied him, often changing his
direction, so that they wondered whither he was leading
them, and began to question him.   But he answered
that he had heard secretly of a great spoil to be taken,
and that they should all have a share of it, and whenever they came upon Arabs of another tribe Abdullah
invited the sheikh and the most notable men to his
tent and entertained them sumptuously with camel's
meat, afterwards talking long with them in private.
Before many weeks had passed, the skilful men of the
tribe, who knew the signs, were aware that many other
Bedouins were travelling in the same direction as
themselves, though they could not be seen.

But neither Abdullah's men, nor Almasta herself, could know that in three months the sheikhs of all the tribes from Hasa to Harb, and from Ajman to El Kora, had heard that Khaled the Sultan was a Persian robber, and a Shiyah at heart, venerating Ali and execrating the true Sonna, a man who in all probability drank wine in secret, and who was certainly plotting to deliver up all Nejed to the power of the Ajjem. Some of them believed the tale readily enough, for all had asked whence Khaled was and none had got an answer. Could a man be of the desert, they asked, and yet not be known by name in any of the tribes, nor his father before him ? Surely, there was a secret, they said, and he who will not tell the name of his father has a reason for changing his own. And as for his being brave and having fought well in the war with the Shammar, how could a man have been a robber if he were not brave, and why should he not fight manfully, since he had everything to gain and nothing to lose ? As for the spoils, too, he had made a pretence of dividing them justly, but it was now well known that he had laden camels by stealth at Haïl and had sent them secretly to Riad, slaughtering with his own hand all those who had helped him.

Little by little, too, the story came to Riad and was told in a low voice by merchants in the bazar, and repeated by their wives among their acquaintance, and by the slaves in the market and among the beggars who begged by the doors of the great mosque but were fed daily from the palace.   And though many persons of the better sort thought that the story might be true, and wagged their heads when Khaled's name was spoken, yet the beggars with one accord declared that it was a lie.   For Khaled was generous in almsgiving, and they said, 'If Khaled is overthrown and another Sultan set up in his place, how do we know whether there will be boiled camel's meat from time to time as well as blanket-bread and a small measure of barley meal?   And will the next Sultan scatter gold in the streets as Khaled did on the first day when he rode to the mosque?   Truly these chatterers of Bedouins talk much of the treasure in the palace which will be divided, but they who talk most of gold, are they who most desire it, and we shall get none.   Therefore we say it is a lie, and Khaled is a true man, and a Sonna like ourselves, not a swiller of wine nor a devourer of pigs.   Allah show him mercy now and at the day of resurrection!   The cock-sparrow is pluming his breast while the hunter is pulling the string of the snare.'

Thus the beggars talked among themselves all day, reasoning after the manner of their kind.   But they suffered other people to talk as they pleased, for one who desires alms must not exhibit a contradictory disposition, lest the rich man be offended and eat the melon together with the melon peels, and exclaim that the dirt-scraper has become a preacher. For the rich man's anger is at the edge of his nostrils and always ready.

As the winter passed away and the spring began, the tribes of the desert drew nearer and nearer to the city, as is their wont at that season. For many of the sheikhs had houses in the city, in which they spent the hot months of the year, while their people were encamped in the low hill country not far off, where the heat is less fierce than in the plains and the deserts. And now also the season of the Haj was approaching, for Ramadhan was not far off, and the beggars congregated at the gates waiting for the first pilgrims, and expecting plentiful alms, which in due time they received, for in that year Abdullah did not molest the Persian pilgrimage, his mind being occupied with other matters.

CHAPTER IX

THE story which was thus repeated from mouth to mouth in Riad reached the palace at the last, and the guards told it to each other as they sat together under the shadow of the great wall, the cooks related it among themselves in the kitchen, and the black slaves gossiped about it in the corners of the courtyard, and the women slaves stood and listened while they talked and carried the tale into the harem. But the people of the palace were more slow to believe than the people of the city, for they shared in a measure in Khaled's right of possession, and desired no change of master, so that for a long time neither Zehowah nor Khaled heard anything of what was commonly reported. Yet at last the old woman who had been Zehowah's nurse told her the substance of the story, with many protestations of unbelief, and of anger against those who had invented the lie.

'It is right that my lady and mistress should know these things,' she said, 'and when our lord the Sultan has been informed of them, he will doubtless cause his

soldiers to go forth with sticks and purify the hides of
the chief evil-speakers in the bazar. There is one
especially, a merchant whose shop is opposite the door
of the little mosque, who is continually bold in falsehood, being the same who sold me this garment for
linen; but it afterwards turned out to be cotton and
the gold threads are brass and have turned black. I
pray Allah to be just as well as merciful.'

At first Zehowah laughed, but soon afterwards her
face became grave, and she bent her brows, for though
the story was but a lie she saw how easily it would
find credence. She therefore sent the old woman
away with a gift and she herself went to Khaled, and
sat down beside him and took his hand.

'You have secret enemies,' she said, 'who are
plotting against your life, and who have already begun
to attack you by filling the air of the city with falsehoods which fly from house to house like flies in summer
entering at the window and going out by the door. You
must sift this matter, for it is worthy of attention.'

'And what are these lies of which you speak?'

'It is said openly in the city that you are a Shiyah
and a Persian, having been a robber before you came
here, and that you are plotting to deliver over Nejed to
the Persians. Look to this, Khaled, for they say
that you are no Bedouin since no one knows your
descent nor the name of your father.'

'Do you believe this of me, Zehowah?' Khaled asked.

'Do I believe that the sun is black and the night as white as the sun? But it is true that I do not know your father's name.'

Then Khaled was troubled, for he saw that it would be a hard matter to explain, and that without explanation his safety might be endangered. Zehowah sat still beside him, holding his hand and looking into his face, as though expecting an answer.

'Have I done wisely in telling you?' she asked at last. 'You are troubled. I should have said nothing.'

'You have done wisely,' he answered. 'For I will go and speak to them, and if they believe me, the matter is finished, but if not I have lost nothing.'

'It will be well to give the chief men presents, and to distribute something among the people, for gifts are great persuaders of unbelief.'

'Shall I give them presents because they have believed evil of me?' asked Khaled, laughing. 'Rather would I give you the treasures of the whole earth because you have not believed it.'

'If I had the wealth of the whole world I would give it to them rather than that they should hurt a hair of your head,' Zehowah answered.

'Am I more dear to you than so much gold, Zehowah?'

'What is gold that it should be weighed in the balance with the life of a man? You are dearer to me than gold.'

'Is this love, Zehowah?' Khaled asked, in a low voice.

'I do not know whether it be love or not.'

'The wing of night is lifted for a moment, and the false dawn is seen, and afterwards it is night again. But the true dawn will come by and by, when night folds her wings before the day.'

'You speak in a riddle, Khaled.'

'It is no matter. I will neither make a speech to the people, nor give them gifts. What is it to me? Let them chatter from the first call to prayer until the lights are put out in the evening. My fate is about my neck, and I cannot change it, any more than I can make you love me. Allah is great. I will wait and see what happens.'

'Everything is undoubtedly in Allah's hand,' said Zehowah. 'But if a man, having meat set before him, will not raise his right hand to thrust it into the dish, he will die of hunger.'

'And do you think that Allah does not know before whether the man will stretch out his hand or not?'

'Undoubtedly Allah knows. And he also knows that if you will not sift this matter and stop the mouths of the liars, I will, though I am but a woman, for otherwise we may both perish.'

'If they destroy me, yet they cannot take the kingdom from you, nor hurt you,' said Khaled. 'How then are you in danger? If I am slain you will then choose a husband, whose father's name is known to them. They will be satisfied and you will be no worse off than before and possibly better. This is truth. I will therefore wait for the end.'

'Who has put these words into your mouth, Khaled? For the thought is not in your heart. Moreover, if the tribes should rise up and overthrow you, they would not spare me, for I would fight against them with my hands and they would kill me.'

'Why should you fight for me, since you do not love me? But this is folly. No one ever heard of a woman taking arms and fighting.'

'I have heard of such deeds. And if I had not heard of them, others should through me, for I would be the first to do them.'

'I think that so long as Khaled lives, Zehowah need not bear arms,' said Khaled. 'I will therefore go and call the chief men together and speak to them.'

And so he did. When the principal officers who had remained in the city during the winter season were assembled in the kahwah, and had hung up their swords on the pegs and partaken of a refreshment, Khaled sent the slaves away, and spoke in a few words as was his manner.

'Men of Riad, Aared and all Nejed,' he said, 'I regret that more of you are not present here, but a great number of sheikhs are still in the desert, and it cannot be helped. I desire to tell you that I have heard of a tale concerning me which is circulated from mouth to ear throughout Riad and the whole kingdom. This tale is untrue, a lie such as no honest man repeats even to his own wife at home in the harem. For it is said that I am not called Khaled, but perhaps Ali Hassan, or perhaps Ali Hussein, that I am a Shiyah, a wine-bibber and an idolatrous one who prays for the intercession of Ali, besides being a Persian and a robber. It is also said that I plot to deliver over the kingdom of Nejed to the Persians, though how this could be done I do not know, seeing that the Persians are a meal-faced people of white jackals who do not know how to ride a camel. These are all lies. I swear by Allah.'

When the men heard these words, they looked stealthily one at another, to see who would answer Khaled, for they had all heard the story and most of them were inclined to believe it. Peace is the mother of evil-speaking, as garbage breeds flies in a corner, which afterwards fly into clean houses and men ask whence they come. But none of the chief men found anything to say at first, so that Khaled sat in silence a long time, waiting for some one to speak. He therefore turned to the one nearest to him, and addressed him.

'Have you heard this tale?' he inquired. 'And if you have heard it do you believe it?'

'I think, indeed, that I have heard something of the kind,' answered the man. 'But it was as the chattering of an uncertain vision in a dream, which rings in the ears for a moment while it is yet dark in the morning, but is forgotten when the sun rises. By the instrumentality of a just mind Allah caused that which entered at one ear to run out from the other as the rinsing of a water-skin.'

'Good,' answered Khaled. 'Yet it is not well to rinse the brains with falsehoods. And you?' he inquired, turning to the next. 'Have you heard it also?'

'Just lord, I have heard,' replied this one. 'But if I have believed, may my head be shaved with a red-hot razor having a jagged edge.'

'This is well,' Khaled said, and he questioned a third.

'O Khaled!' cried the man. 'Is the milk sour, because the slave has imagined a lie saying, "I will say it is bad and then it will be given to me to drink"?

N

Or is honey bitter because the cook has put salt in the
sweetmeats ?   Or is it night because the woman has
shut the door and the window, to keep out the sun ?'

The next also found an answer, having collected
his thoughts while the others were speaking.

'A certain man,' said he, 'kept sheep in Tabal
Shammar, and the dog was with the sheep in the fold.
Then two foxes came to the fold in the evening and
one of them said to the man: "All dogs are wolves,
for we have seen their like in the mountains, and your
dog is also a wolf and will eat up your sheep.   Make
haste to kill him therefore and cast out his carcass."
And to the sheep the other fox said: "How many
sheep hang by the heels at the butcher's !   And how
many dogs live in sheepfolds !   This is an evil world for
innocent people."   And the sheep were at first persuaded, but presently the dog ran out and caught one
of the foxes and broke his neck, and the man threw a
stone at the other and hit him, so that he also died.
Then the sheep said one to another: "The foxes have
suffered justly, for they were liars and robbers and the
dog and our master have protected us against them,
which they would not have done had they desired our
destruction."   And so are the people, O Khaled.   For
if you let the liars go unhurt the people will believe
them, but if you destroy them the faith of the multitude
will be turned again to you.'

'This is a fable,' said Khaled, 'and it is not without truth. I am the sheep-dog and the people are
the sheep. But in the name of Allah, which are the
foxes?'

Then he turned to another, an old man who was
the Kadi, celebrated for his wisdom and for his
religious teaching in the chief mosque.

'I ask you last of all,' said Khaled, 'because you
are the wisest, and when the wisest words are heard
last they are most easily remembered. For we first
put water into the lamp, and then oil to float upon
the surface, and next the wick, and last of all we take
a torch and light the lamp and the darkness dis-
appears. Light our lamp, therefore, O Kadi, and
let us see clearly.'

'O Khaled,' replied the Kadi, 'I am old and
have seen the world. You cannot destroy the tree by
cutting off one or two of its branches. It is necessary
to strike at the root. Now the root of this tree of
lies which has grown up is this. Neither we nor the
people know whence you are, nor what was your
father's name, and though I for my part do not im-
piously ask whence Allah takes the good gifts which
he gives to men, there are many who are not satisfied,
and who will go about in jealousy to make trouble
until their questioning is answered. If you ask
counsel of me, I say, tell us here present of what

tribe you are, for we believe you a pure Bedouin like the best of us, and tell us your father's name, and peace be upon him. We are men in authority and will speak to the people, and I will address them from the pulpit of the great mosque, and they will believe us. Then all will be ended, and the lies will be extinguished as the coals of an evening fire go out when the night frost descends upon the camp in winter. But if you will not tell us, yet I, for one, do not believe ill of you; and moreover you are lord, and we are vassals, so long as you are King and hold good and evil in your hand.'

'So long as I am King,' Khaled repeated. 'And you think that if I do not tell my father's name, I shall not be where I am for a long time.'

'Allah is wise, and knows,' answered the Kadi, but he would say nothing more.

'This is plain speaking,' said Khaled, 'such as I like. But I might plainly take advantage of it. You desire to know my father's name and whence I come. Then is it not easy for me to say that I come from a distant part of the Great Dahna? Is there a man in Nejed who has crossed the Red Desert? And if I say that my father was Mohammed ibn Abd el Hamid ibn Abd el Latif, and so on to our father Ismaïl, upon whom be peace, shall any one deny that I speak truth? This is a very easy matter.'

'So much the more will it be easy for us to satisfy the people,' answered the Kadi.

'No doubt. I will think of what you have said. And now, I pray you, partake of another refreshment and go in peace.'

At this all the chief men looked one at the other again, for they saw that Khaled would not tell them what they wished to know. And those of them who had doubted the story before now began to believe it. But they held their peace, and presently made their salutation and took their swords from the wall and departed.

Khaled then left the kahwah and returned to Zehowah in the harem.

'I have told them that these tales are lies,' he said, 'but they do not believe me.'

He repeated to Zehowah all that had been said, and she listened attentively, for she began to understand that there was danger not far off.

'And I told them,' he said at last, 'that it would be as easy for me to invent names, as for them to hear them. Then they looked sideways each at the other and kept silent.'

'This is a foolish thing which you have done,' answered Zehowah. 'They will now all believe that your father was an evildoer and that you yourself are no better. Otherwise, they will say, why should he wish to conceal anything ?   You should have told them the truth, whatever it is.'

'You also wish to know it, I see,' said Khaled, looking at Zehowah curiously. 'But if I were to tell you, you would not believe me, I think, any more than they would.'

Then Zehowah looked at him in her turn, but he could not understand the language of her eyes.

'What is this secret of yours ?' she asked. 'I would indeed like to hear it, and if you swear to me that it is true, by Allah, I will believe you.   For you are a very truthful man, and not subtle.'

But Khaled was troubled at this.   For he knew that she would find it hard to believe ; and that if she did believe it, she would be terrified to think that she had married one of the genii, and if not, she would suspect him of a hidden purpose in telling her an empty fable, and he would then be further from her love than before.   He held his peace, therefore, for some time, while she watched him, playing with her beads.   In reality she was very curious to know the truth, though she had always been unwilling to ask it of him, seeing that she had married him as a stranger, of her own will and choice, without inquiry.

'Is it just,' she asked at last, 'that the people should accuse you of evil deeds and fill the air of the city with falsehoods concerning you, so that the very

slaves hear the guards repeating the lies to each other
in the courtyard, and that I, who am your wife, should
not know the truth? What have I done that you
should not trust me? Or what have I said that you
should regard me no more than a slave who sprinkles
the floor and makes the fire, and while she is present
in the room you hold your peace lest she should know
your thoughts and betray them? Am I not your
wife, and faithful? Have I not given you a kingdom
and treasure beyond counting? .Surely there were
times when you talked more freely with that barbarian
slave-woman, whose hair was red, than you ever talk
with me.'

'This is not true,' said Khaled. 'And if I talked
familiarly with Almasta, you know the reason, for you
yourself found it out, and called me simple for trying
to deceive you. And now she is gone to the desert
with her husband and there is no more question of her,
or her red hair. But all the rest is true, and you have
indeed given me a kingdom, which I am likely to lose
and wealth which I do not desire, though you have not
given me that which I covet more than gold or kingdoms, for I desire it indeed, and that is your love.
Moreover if you have given me the rest, I have done
something in return, for I have fought for your people,
and shed my blood freely, and given you a nation captive, besides loving you and refusing to take another

wife into my house. And this last is a matter of which some women would think more highly than you.'

But Zehowah's curiosity was burning within her like a thirst, for although she had at first cared little to know of Khaled's former life, she was astonished at his persistency in keeping the secret now, seeing that the whole country was full of false rumours about him.

'How can a man expect that a woman should love him, if he will not put his trust in her?' she asked.

Then Khaled did not hesitate any longer, for he was never slow to do anything by which there seemed to be any hope of gaining her love. He therefore took her hand in his, and it trembled a little so that he was pleased, though indeed the unsteadiness came more from her anxiety to know the story he was about to tell, than from any love she felt at that moment.

'You have sworn that you will believe me, Zehowah,' he said. 'But I forewarn you that there are hard things to understand. For the reason why I will not tell my father's name, nor the name of my tribe is a plain one, seeing that I was not born like other men, and have no father at all, and my brethren are not men but genii of the air, created from the beginning and destined to die at the second blast of the trumpet before the resurrection of the dead.'

At this Zehowah started suddenly in fright and

looked into his face, expecting to see that he had coals
of fire for eyes and an appalling countenance.   But
when she saw that he was not changed and had the
face of a man and the eyes of a man, she laughed.

'What is this idle tale of Afrits?' she exclaimed.
'Frighten children with it.'

'This is what I foresaw in you,' said Khaled.
'You cannot believe me.   Of what use is it then to
tell you my story?'

Zehowah answered nothing, for she was angry,
supposing that Khaled was attempting to put her off
with a foolish tale.   She had heard, indeed, of Genii and
Afrits and she was sure that they had existence, since
they were expressly mentioned in the Koran, but she
had never heard that any of them had taken the shape
and manner of a man.   She remembered also how
Khaled had always fought with his hands in war, like
other men and been wounded, and she was sure that if
his story were true he would have summoned whole
legions of his fellows through the air to destroy the
enemy.

'You do not believe me,' he repeated somewhat
bitterly.   'And if you do not believe me, how shall
others do so?'

'You ask me to believe too much.   If you ask for
my faith, you must offer me truths and not fables.   It
is true that I am curious, which is foolish and womanly.

But if you do not wish to tell me your secret, I cannot force you to do so, nor have I any right to expect confidence. Let us therefore talk of other things, or else not talk at all, for though you will not satisfy me you cannot deceive me in this way.'

'So you also believe that I am a Persian and a robber,' said Khaled. 'Is it not so?'

'How can I tell what you are, if you will not tell me? Is your name written in your face that I may know it is indeed Khaled and not Ali Hassan as the people say? Or is the record of your deeds inscribed upon your forehead for me to read? You may be a Persian. I cannot tell.'

Then Khaled bent his brows and turned his eyes away from her, for he was angry and disappointed, though indeed she knew in her heart that he was no Persian. But she let him suppose that she thought so, hoping perhaps to goad him into satisfying her curiosity.

If Khaled had been a man like other men, as Zehowah supposed him to be, he would doubtless have invented a well-framed history such as she would have believed, at least for the present. But to him such a falsehood appeared useless, for he had seen the world during many ages and had observed that a lie is never really successful except by chance, seeing that no intelligence is profound enough to foresee the manner in which it will be some day examined, whereas the truth, being always coincident with the reality, can never be wholly refuted.

Khaled therefore hesitated as to whether he should tell his story from the beginning, or hold his peace; but in the end he decided to speak, because it was intolerable to him to be thought an evildoer by her.

'You make haste to disbelieve, before you have heard all,' he said at last. 'Hear me to the end. I have told you that I slew the Indian prince. That was before I became a man. You yourself could not understand how I was able to enter the palace and carry him away without being observed. But as I was at that time able to fly and to make both myself and him invisible, this need not surprise you. If you do not believe that I did it, let us order a litter to be brought for you, and I will take my mare and a sufficient number of attendants, and let us ride southwards into the Red Desert. There I will show you the man's bones. You will probably recognise them by the gold chain which he wore about his neck and by his ring. After that, when I had buried him, the messenger of Allah came to me, and because the man was an unbeliever, and had intended to embrace the faith outwardly, having evil in his heart, Allah did not destroy me immediately, but commanded that the angel Asrael should write my name in the book of

life, that I might become a man.   But Allah gave me
no soul, promising only that if I could win your love,
whose suitor I had killed, I should receive an immortal spirit, which should then be judged according
to my deeds.   This is truth.   I swear it in the name
of Allah, the merciful, the compassionate.   Then an
angel gave me garments such as men wear, and a
sword, and a good mare, and I travelled hither to
Riad, eating locusts for food.   And though no man
knew me, you married me at once, for it was the will of
Allah, whose will shall also be done to the end.   The
rest you know.   If, therefore, you will love me before
I die, I shall receive a soul and it may be that I shall
inherit paradise, for I am a true believer and have
shed blood for the faith.   But if you do not love me,
when I die I shall perish as the flame of a lamp that
is blown out at dawn.   This is the truth.'

He ceased from speaking and looked again at
Zehowah.   At first he supposed from her face that
she believed him, and his heart was comforted, but
presently she smiled, and he understood that she was
not convinced.   For the story had interested her
greatly and she had almost forgotten not to believe it,
but when she no longer heard his voice, it seemed too
hard for her.

'This is a strange tale,' she said, 'and it will
probably not satisfy the people.'

'I do not care whether they are satisfied or not,' Khaled answered. 'All I desire is to be believed by you, for I cannot bear that you should think me what I am not.'

'What can I do ?   I cannot say to my intelligence, take this and reject that, any more than I can say to my heart, love or love not.   It would indeed have been easier if you had said, "I am a certain Persian, a fugitive, protect me, for my enemies are upon me." I could perhaps give you protection if you require it, as you may.   But you come to me with a monstrous tale, and you ask me to love, not a man, but a Jinn or an Afrit, or whatever it pleases you to call yourself. Assuredly this is too hard for me.'

And again Zehowah smiled scornfully, for she was really beginning to think that he might be a Persian disguised as the people said.

'I need no protection from man or woman,' said Khaled, 'for I fear neither the one nor the other. For I am strong, and if I am able to give out of charity I am also able to take by force.   My fate is ever with me.   I cannot escape it.   But neither can others escape theirs.   I will fight alone if need be, for if you will not love me I care little how I may end.   Moreover, in battle, it is not good to stand in the way of a man who seeks death.'

But Zehowah thought this might be the speech of

a desperate man such as Ali Hassan, the robber, as well as of Khaled, the Jinn, and she was not convinced, though she no longer smiled. For she knew little of supernatural beings, and a devil might easily call himself a good spirit, so that she was convinced that she was married either to a demon or to a dangerous robber, and she could not even decide which of the two she would have preferred, for either was bad enough, and as for love there could no longer be any question of that.

Khaled understood well enough and rose from his seat and went away, desiring to be alone. He knew that he was now surrounded by danger on every side and that he could not even look to his wife for comfort, since she also believed him to be an impostor.

'Truly,' he said to himself, 'this is a task beyond accomplishment, which Allah has laid upon me. It is harder to get a woman's love than to win kingdoms, and it is easier to destroy a whole army with one stroke of a sword than to make a woman believe that which she does not desire. And now the end is at hand. For she will never love me and I shall certainly perish in this fight, being alone against so many. Allah assuredly did not intend me to run away, and moreover there is no reason left for remaining alive.'

On that day Khaled again called the chief men together in his kahwah, and addressed them briefly.

'Men of Riad,' he said, 'I am aware that there is a conspiracy to overthrow and destroy me, and I daresay that you yourselves are among the plotters. I will not tell you who I am, but I swear by Allah that I am neither a Persian nor a robber, nor yet a Shiyah. You will doubtless attack me unawares, but you will not find me sleeping. I will kill as many of you as I can, and afterwards I also shall undoubtedly be killed, for I am alone and you have many thousands on your side. Min Allah—it is in Allah's hands. Go in peace.'

So they departed, shaking their heads, but saying nothing.

CHAPTER X

THE Sheikh of the beggars was an old man, blind from
his childhood, but otherwise strong and full of health,
delighting in quarrels and swift to handle his staff.
He had at first become a beggar, being still a young
man, for his father and mother had died without
making provision for him, and he had no brothers.
As he boasted that he was of the pure blood of the
desert on both sides, the other beggars jeered at him
in the beginning, calling him Ibn el Sheikh in derision and sometimes stealing his food from him. But
he beat them mightily, the just and the unjust
together, since he could not see, and acquired great
consideration amongst them, after which he behaved
generously, giving his share with the rest for the
common good, and something more. His companions
learned also that his story was true and that his
blood was as good as any from Ajman To El Kara, for
a Bedouin of the same tribe as Abdullah, the husband
of Almasta, came to see him not less than once every
year, and called him brother and filled his sack with

barley. This Bedouin was a person of consideration, also, as the beggars saw from his having a mare of his own, provided with a good saddle, and from his weapons. In the course of time therefore the blind man grew great in the eyes of his fellows, until they called him Sheikh respectfully, and waited on him when he performed his ablutions, and he obtained over them a supremacy as great as was Khaled's over the kingdom he governed. He was very wise also, acquainted with the interpretation of dreams, and able to recite various chapters of the Koran. It was even said that he was able to distinguish a good man from a bad by the sound of his tread, though some thought that he only heard the jingling of coins in the girdle, and judged by this, having a finer hearing than other men. At all events he was often aware that a person able to give alms was approaching, while his companions were talking among themselves and noticed nothing, though they had eyes to see, being mostly only cripples and lepers.

On a certain day in the spring, when the sun was beginning to be hot and not long after Khaled had told Zehowah his story, many of the beggars were sitting in the eastern gate, by which the great road issues out of the city towards Hasa. They expected the coming of the first pilgrims every day, for the season was advancing. And now they sat talking

O

together of the good prospects before them, and re-
joicing that the winter was over so that they would
not suffer any more from the cold.

'There is a horseman on the road,' said the Sheikh
of the beggars, interrupting the conversation. 'O you
to whom Allah has preserved the light of day, look
forth and tell me who the rider is.'

'It is undoubtedly a pilgrim,' answered a young
beggar, who was a stranger but had found his way to
Riad without legs, no man knew how.

'Ass of Egypt,' replied the Sheikh reprovingly, 'do
pilgrims ride at a full gallop upon steeds of pure
blood? But though your eyes are open your ears are
deaf with the sleep of stupidity from which there is no
awakening. That is a good horse, ridden by a light
rider. Truly a man must itch to be called Haji who
gallops thus on the road to Mecca.'

Then the others looked, and at last one of them
spoke, a hunchback having but one eye, but that one
was keen.

'O Sheikh,' he said, 'rejoice and praise Allah, for I
think it is he whom you call your brother, who comes
in from the desert to visit you.'

'If that is the case, I will indeed give thanks,'
answered the blind man, 'for there is little in my
barley-sack, less in my wallet and nothing at all in
my stomach. Allah is gracious and compassionate!'

The hunchback's eye had not deceived him, and before long the Bedouin dismounted at the gate and looked about until he saw the Sheikh of the beggars, who indeed had already risen to welcome him. When they had embraced the Bedouin led the blind man along in the shadow of the eastern wall until they were so far from the rest that they might freely talk without being overheard. Then they sat down together, and the mare stood waiting before them.

'O my brother,' the Bedouin began, 'was not my mother the adopted daughter of your uncle, upon whom be peace ? And have I not called you brother and filled your barley-sack from time to time these many years ?'

'This is true,' answered the Sheikh of the beggars. 'Allah will requite you with seventy thousand days of unspeakable bliss for every grain of barley you have caused to pass my teeth. "Be constant in prayer and in giving alms," says the holy book, "and you shall find with Allah all the good which you have sent before you, for your souls." And it is also said, "Give alms to your kindred, and to the poor and to orphans." I am also grateful for all you have done, and my gratitude grows as a palm tree in the garden of my soul which is irrigated by your charity.'

'It is well, my brother, it is well. I know the uprightness of your heart, and I have not ridden hither from the desert to count the treasure which

may be in store for me in paradise. Allah knows the
good, as well as the evil. I have come for another
purpose. But tell me first, what is the news in the
city? Are there no strange rumours afloat of late
concerning Khaled the Sultan?'

'In each man's soul there are two wells,' said the
blind man. 'The one is the spring of truth, the other
is the fountain of lies.'

'You are wise and full of years,' said the Bedouin,
'and I understand your caution, for I also am not
very young. But here we must speak plainly, for the
time is short in which to act. A sand-storm has
darkened the eyes of the men of the desert and they
are saying that Khaled is a Shiyah, a Persian and a
robber, and that he must be overthrown and a man of
our own people made king in his stead.'

'I have indeed heard such a rumour.'

'It is more than a rumour. The tribes are even
now assembling towards Riad, and before many days
are past the end will come. Abdullah is the chief
mover in this. But with your help, my brother, we
will make his plotting empty and his scheming fruit-
less as a twig of ghada stuck into the sand, which will
neither strike root nor bear leaves.'

When the Sheikh of the beggars heard that he was
expected to give help in frustrating Abdullah's plans
he was troubled and much astonished.

'Shall the blind sheep go out and fight the lion?'
he inquired tremulously.

'Even so,' replied the Bedouin unmoved, 'and,
moreover, without danger to himself. Hear me first.
Abdullah and his tribe will encamp in the low hills, in
a few days, as usual, but somewhat earlier than in
other years, and a great number of other Bedouins will
be in the neighbouring valleys at the same time.
Then Abdullah will come into the city openly and go
to his house with his wife and slaves, and during
several days he will receive the visits of his friends and
return them, and go to the palace and salute Khaled,
as though nothing were about to happen. But in the
meantime he will make everything ready, for it is his
intention to go into the palace at night, disguised in
a woman's garment, with his wife, and they will slay
Khaled in his sleep, and bind Zehowah, and distribute
much treasure among the guards and slaves, and before
morning the city will be full of Bedouins all ready to
proclaim Abdullah Sultan. And you alone can prevent
all this.'

But the blind man laughed in his beard.

'This is a good jest!' he cried. 'You have sought
out a valiant warrior to stand between the Sultan and
death! I am blind and old, and a beggar, and you
would have me stand in the path of Abdullah and a
thousand armed men. They would certainly laugh, as

I do. Let me take with me a few lepers and the Egyptian jackass without legs, who has flown among us lately like a locust out of the clear air. Verily, their strength shall avail against the lances of the desert.'

'This is no jest, my brother,' answered the Bedouin, gravely. 'Neither I, nor a hundred armed horsemen with me could do what you will do unhurt. But I will save Khaled. For in the battle of the pass before we came to Haïl last summer when I had an arrow in my right arm and a spear thrust in my side, certain dogs of Shammars encompassed me, and darkness was already descending upon my eyes when Khaled rode in like a whirlwind of scythes, and sent four of them to hell, where they are now drinking molten brass like thirsty camels. Then I swore by Allah that I would defend him in the hour of need.'

'Why do you not then lie in wait for Abdullah yourself and slay him as he passes you in the dark?'

'Is he not the sheikh of my tribe? How then can I lay a hand on him? But I have thought of this during many nights in my tent, and you alone can do what is needed.'

'Surely this is folly,' said the Sheikh of the beggars. 'You have met a hot wind in the desert and your mind is unsettled by it. I pray you come with me into the city to my dwelling, and take some refreshment, or at least let me send to the well for a drink of water.'

'My head is cool and I am not thirsty, nor is the hot wind blowing at this time of year. Hear me. I will tell you how to save Khaled from destruction, and you shall receive more gold than you have dreamed of, and a house, and rich garments, and a young wife of a good family to comfort your old age. For the deed is easy and safe, but the reward will be great, and you alone can do the one and earn the other.'

'I perceive,' said the blind man, 'that you are indeed in earnest, but I cannot understand what I can do. We know that Khaled is forewarned, for it is not many days since he summoned the chief men in Riad, with the Kadi, to the palace, and refused to tell them the name of his father, but said that if they attacked him he would kill as many of them as he could.'

'I did not know this,' answered the Bedouin. 'But the knowledge does not change my plan. Now hear me. You are the Sheikh of all the beggars in Riad—may Allah send you long life and much gain —they are an army and you are a captain. Moreover the beggars are doubtless attached to Khaled by his generosity, and all of you say in your hearts that under Abdullah there may be more sticks and less barley for you.'

'This is true. But then, my brother, it is other-wise with you, for you are of Abdullah's tribe and will have honour and riches if he is made Sultan. How then is my advantage also yours?'

'And did not this Abdullah in the first place divorce with ignominy his second wife, who is my kinswoman, being the daughter of my father's sister? And has he restored the dowry as the law commands? Truly his new wife is even now sitting upon my cousin's carpet. And secondly Abdullah made himself sheikh unjustly, for our sheikh should be Abdul Kerim's son.'

'Yet you accepted Abdullah and promised him allegiance.'

'Does the camel say to his driver: "I do not like to carry a load of barley, I would rather bear a basket of dates"? "Eat what you please in your tent, but dress as other men," says the proverb. Hear me, for I speak wisdom. Abdullah will come into the city and go to his house, intending to prepare the way for evil. And he will walk about the streets as usual, without attendants, both because he knows that the people are mostly with him, and also in order not to attract notice. Now Abdullah is the spring from which all this wickedness flows, he is the chief camel whom the others follow, the coal in the ashes by which the fire is kept alive, the head without which the body cannot live. Dry up the spring, therefore, let the chief camel fall into a pit suddenly, extinguish the coal, strike off

the head.   Let them ask.in the morning : " Where is
he ? "   And let him not be found anywhere.   Then
the people will be amazed and will not know what to
do, having no leader.   This is for you to do, and it
can easily be done.'

'What folly is this ? ' asked the blind man, shaking
his head.   'And how can I do what you wish ? '

'It is very easy, for I know that you and your
companions are as one man, living together for the
common good.   Go to the beggars therefore and tell
them what I have told you, and be not afraid, for
they will not betray you.   And when Abdullah walks
about the city alone lie in wait for him, for you will
easily catch him in a narrow street, and two or three
score of you can run after him begging for alms, until
he is surrounded on all sides.   Then fall upon him,
and bind him, and take him secretly to one of your
dwellings and keep him there, so that none find him,
until the storm is past.   In this way you will save
Khaled and the kingdom, and when all is quiet you
can deliver him up to be a laughing-stock at the
palace and to all who believed in him.   For there is
nothing to fear, and I, for my part, am sure that
Abdul Kerim's son will immediately be made sheikh
of our tribe so that Abdullah will not return to us.'

'You are subtle, my brother,' said the Sheikh of
the beggars, smiling and stroking his beard.   'This is

a good plan, being very simple, and Khaled will be grateful to us, and honour us beggars exceedingly. Said I not well that the jest was good? Surely it is better than I had thought, and more profitable.'

'I have thought of it long in the nights of winter, both by the camp fire and in my tent and on the march. But I have told no one, nor will tell any one until all is done. But so soon as you have taken Abdullah and hidden him, let me know of it. To this end, when we are encamped outside the city I will come every evening to prayers in the great mosque and afterwards will wait for you near the door. As soon as I know that Abdullah is out of finding I will spread the report that he is lost, and before long all our tribe will give up the search, being indeed glad to get rid of him. And the rest is in the hand of Allah. I have done what I can, you must now do your share.'

'By Allah! You shall not complain of me,' answered the blind man, 'nor of my people, for the jest is surpassingly good, and shall be well carried out.'

'I will therefore go into the city, where I have business,' said the Bedouin. 'For I gave a reason for coming alone to Riad, and must needs show myself there to those who know me.'

So the Bedouin filled the blind beggar's sack with barley and dates from his own supply and embraced him and went into the city, but the Sheikh of the beggars remained sitting in the same place for some time, at a distance from the rest, in an attitude of inward contemplation, though he was in reality listening to what the hunchback was telling the new cripple from Egypt. The Sheikh's ears were sharper than those of other men and he heard very clearly what was said.

'This Bedouin,' said the hunchback, 'is a near relation of our Sheikh, and holds him in great veneration, coming frequently to see him even from a considerable distance, and always bringing him a present of food. And you may see by his mare and by his weapons that he is a person of consideration in his tribe. For our Sheikh is not a negro, nor the son of a Syrian camel-driver, but an Arab of the best blood in the desert, and wise enough to sit in the council in the Sultan's palace. You, who are but lately arrived, being transported into our midst by the mercy of Allah, must learn all these things, and you will also find out that our Sheikh has eyes in his ears, and in his fingers and in his staff, though he is counted blind, and you cannot deceive him easily as you might suppose.'

The Sheikh of the beggars was pleased when he heard this and listened attentively to hear the answer made by the Egyptian, whom he did not yet trust because he was a newcomer and a stranger.

'Truly,' replied the cripple, 'Allah has been merci-

ful and compassionate to me, for he has brought me
into the society of the wise and the good, which is
better than much feasting in the company of the
ignorant and the ill-mannered. And as for the Sheikh,
he is evidently a very holy man, to whom eyes are not
in any way necessary, his inward sight being constantly fixed upon heavenly things.'

This answer did not altogether please the blind man,
for it savoured somewhat of flattery. But the other
beggars approved of the speech, deeming that it showed
a submissive spirit, and readiness to obey and respect
their chief.

'O you of Egypt!' cried the Sheikh, calling to him.
'Come here and sit beside me, for I have heard what
you said and desire your company.'

The cripple immediately began to crawl along by
the wall, dragging himself upon his hands and body,
for he had no legs.

'He is obedient,' thought the blind man, 'though it
costs him much labour to move.'

When the man was beside him, the Sheikh took an
onion and a date from his wallet and set them down
upon the ground.

'Eat,' he said, 'and give thanks.'

The cripple thanked him and taking the food, began
to eat the onion.

'You have taken the onion in your right hand and

the date in your left,' said the Sheikh. 'And you are eating the onion first.'

'This is true,' answered the Egyptian. 'I see that my lord has indeed eyes in his fingers.'

'I have,' said the Sheikh. 'But that is not all, for this is an allegory. All men like to eat the onion first and the date afterwards, for though the onion be ever so sweet and tender, its taste is bitter when a man has eaten sugar-dates before it. But you have begun by giving us the mellow fruit of flattery, and when you give us the wholesome vegetable of truth it will be too sharp for our palates. Ponder this in your heart, chew it as the camel does her cud, and the well-digested food of wisdom shall nourish your understanding.'

The cripple listened in astonishment at the depth of the Sheikh's thought, and he would have spoken out his admiration, but it is not possible to eat an onion and to be eloquent at the same time. The blind man knew this and continued to give him instruction.

'The onion has saved you,' he said, 'for your mouth being full you could say nothing flattering, and now you will think before you speak. Consider how I have treated you. Have I at once rendered thanks to Allah for sending into our midst a young man whose gifts of eloquence are at least equal to those of the Kadi himself? I have said nothing so foolish. I have called you an ass of Egypt and otherwise rebuked you, for the good of your understanding, though I begin to think that you are indeed a very estimable young man, and it is possible that your wit may ripen in our society. But now I perceive by my hearing that you are eating the date. I pray you now, eat another onion after it.'

'I cannot,' answered the cripple, 'for my lips are puckered at the thought of it.'

'Neither is truth sweet after flattery,' said the Sheikh, who then began to eat the other onion himself.

'I will endeavour to profit by your precepts, my lord,' replied the Egyptian.

'Allah will then certainly enlighten you, my son. Remember also another thing. We are ourselves here a community, distinct from the citizens of Riad, and what we do, we do for the common good. Remember therefore to share what you receive with the rest, as they will share what they have with you, and take part with them in whatsoever is done by common consent. In this way it will be well with you and you shall grow fat; but if you are against us you will find evil in every man's hand, for since it has pleased Allah to give you no legs, you cannot possibly run away.'

Having said this much the Sheikh of the beggars was silent. But afterwards on the same day he gathered about him the strongest of his companions, being mostly men who had the use of both arms and both legs, though some of them were lepers and some had but one eye, and some were deaf and dumb, according to the affliction which it had pleased Allah to send upon each. These were the most trusty and faithful of his people, and to them he communicated openly what the Bedouin had proposed to him in secret. All of them approved the plan, for they greatly feared the overthrow of Khaled.

'But,' said one, 'we cannot keep this Abdullah for ever, and we can surely not kill him, for we should bring upon ourselves a grievous punishment.'

'Allah forbid that we should shed blood,' replied the Sheikh. 'But when Abdul Kerim's son is made Sheikh of the tribe, Abdullah will probably not wish to go back to his people. Moreover it shall be for Khaled to judge what shall be done to the man, and he will probably cut off his head. But in the meantime it is necessary to choose amongst us spies, two for each gate of the city, to the number of twenty-two men, to watch for Abdullah. For we do not know when he will come, and of the two spies who see him enter, both must follow him and see whither he goes, and then the one will immediately inform all the rest while the other waits for him. From the time he enters the city he will not be able to go anywhere without our knowledge, and we shall certainly catch him one day towards dusk in some narrow street of the city.'

The beggars saw that this plan was wise and safe for themselves, and they did as the Sheikh advised, posting men at all the gates to wait for Abdullah. He was, indeed, not far distant, and before many days he rode into the city towards evening, attended by a few slaves and two Bedouins, his wife Almasta riding in the midst of them upon a camel. His face was not hidden and the two beggars who were watching recognised him immediately. They both followed him, until he entered his own house, and then the one sat down in the street to watch until he should come out, asking alms of those who accompanied him, until they also went in, with the beasts. But the other made haste to find the Sheikh and to inform him that Abdullah had come and was now in his own dwelling.

'It is well,' said the blind man. 'The cat is now asleep, and dreams of mice, but he shall wake in the midst of dogs. Abdullah will not leave his house to-night, for it is late, and though he is not afraid in the daytime, he will not go out much at night, lest a secret messenger from Khaled, bearing evil in his hand, should meet him by the way. But to-morrow before dawn, some of us will wait in the neighbour-hood of his house, and two or three score of others feigning to be all blind, as I am, must always be near at hand, watching us. We will then begin to impor-tune him for alms, flattering him with fine language, as though we knew his plans. And this we will do continually, when he is abroad, until one day to escape from us he will turn quickly into a narrow street, supposing that we cannot see him. For he will not wish to be pursued by our cries in the bazar lest he be obliged for shame to give something to each. Then those who can see will open their eyes and we will catch him in the lane, and bind rags over his head so that he cannot cry out, and lead him away to my dwelling by the Yemamah gate. And if any meet us by the way and inquire whom we are taking with us, we will say that he is one of ourselves, who is an epileptic and has fallen down in a fit, and that we are taking him to the farrier's by the gate, to be burned with red-hot irons for his recovery, as the physicians recommend in such cases. Surely we have now foreseen most things, but if we have forgotten anything, Allah will doubtless provide.'

All the beggars in council approved this plan, for they saw that it could be easily carried out, if they could only catch Abdullah in a lonely street at the hour of prayer when few persons are passing.

But Abdullah himself was ignorant of the evil in store for him, and feared nothing, having been secretly informed that most of the better sort of people were ready to support him if he would strike the blow; for they suspected Khaled of being a traitor, especially since he had last addressed the chief men and refused to tell the name of his father. Abdullah therefore came and went openly in the city.

In the meantime, however, Khaled was informed of his presence and was warned of the danger. The aged Kadi came secretly by night to the palace and desired to be received by the Sultan in order to communicate to him news of great importance, as he said. Khaled immediately received him, and the Kadi proceeded to give a full account of Abdullah's designs ; but the Sultan expressed no astonishment.

' Let him do what he will,' he answered, ' for I care little and, after all, what must be will be.'

' But I beseech you to consider,' said the Kadi, ' that by acting promptly you could easily quell this revolution, in which I, by Allah, have no part and will have none. For though many persons may just now desire your overthrow, because they expect to get a share of the treasure in the confusion, yet few are disposed to accept such a man as Abdullah ibn Mohammed el Herir in your place. Even his own tribe are not all faithful to him, and I am credibly informed that many look upon him as an intruder, and would prefer the son of Abdul Kerim for sheikh, as would be just, if the rights of birth were considered. And it would be an easy matter to remove this Abdullah. I implore you to think of the matter.'

'Would this not be a murder?' asked Khaled, looking curiously at the venerable preacher.

'Allah is merciful and forgiving,' replied the old man, looking down and stroking his beard. 'And moreover, if you suffer Abdullah to go about a few days longer he will certainly destroy you, whereas it is an easy matter to give him a cup of such good drink as will save him from thirst ever afterwards, and you would obtain quiet and the kingdom would be at peace.'

'They shall not find me sleeping,' said Khaled, 'and so that I may only slay a score of them first, I care not how soon I perish.'

'This is indeed a new kind of madness!' exclaimed the Kadi. 'I cannot understand it. But I have done what I could, and I can do nothing more.'

'Nor is there anything more to be done,' said Khaled. 'But I thank you, for it is clear that you have spoken from a good intention.'

So the Kadi went away again, and Khaled returned to Zehowah, caring not at all whether he lived or died. But Zehowah began to watch him narrowly.

'If this man were a Persian, an enemy and a traitor,' she thought, 'he would now begin to take measures for his own safety, seeing that he is threatened on every side. Yet he does not lift a hand to defend himself. This can proceed only from one of

two causes.   Either he is a Jinn, as he has told me,
and they cannot kill him, and so he does not fear
them; or else he desires death, out of a sort of madness which has grown up in him through this love of
which he is always speaking.'

CHAPTER XI

IN these days many of the Bedouin tribes came near the city and encamped in great numbers within half a day's journey and less. Abdullah was exceedingly busy with his preparations, and spent much time in talking with other sheikhs, hardly making any concealment of his movements or plans. For by this time it seemed clear to him that the greater part of the people were with him, and every one spoke of the coming overthrow of Khaled as an open matter. Khaled himself, too, was reported to be in fear of his life, and he was no longer seen in the streets as formerly, nor in the courts of the palace, nor even every day in the hall, but remained shut up in the harem, and none saw him except the women and a few slaves. Men said aloud that he was in great fear and distress, and as this story gained credence, so Abdullah's importance increased, since it was he who had brought such terror upon Khaled. All this was open talk in the bazar, but Abdullah was himself somewhat suspicious, supposing that Khaled must have a plan in reserve for defending his possession of the throne. Abdullah, however, kept secret the manner in which he intended to enter the palace, though he promised his adherents to open to them the gates of the castle, and the doors of the treasure chambers on a certain day, which he named, at the time of the first call to prayer in the morning, warning all those who were with him to come together in the great square before that hour in order to be ready to help him, if necessary, and to overwhelm the guards of the palace if they should make any resistance. But he did not know that the man of his tribe who was kinsman to the chief of the beggars had overheard his talk with his wife.

Meanwhile the beggars seemed to be multiplied exceedingly in Riad, for whenever Abdullah went out of his house they came upon him, sometimes by twos and threes and sometimes in scores, pressing close to him and begging alms. They also cried out a great deal, praising his generosity and praying for blessings upon him.

'Behold the sheikh of sheikhs!' they exclaimed. 'He bears gold in his right hand and silver in his left. Yallah! Send him a long life and prosperity, for he loves the poor and his name is the Alms-giver. He is not El Herir but Er Rahman and his heart overflows with mercy as his purse does with small coins.

Come, O brothers, and taste of his charity, which is a perpetual spring of good water beside a palm tree full of sugar-dates! Ya Abdullah, Servant of Allah, we love you! You are our father and mother. Your kefiyeh is the banner which goes before our pilgrimage. Come, O brothers, and taste of his charity.'

Abdullah was not dissatisfied with these words, and the beggars said much more to the same effect, which he regarded as signs of his popularity, so that he opened his purse from time to time and threw handfuls of money into the crowd, not counting the cost since he expected to be master of all the treasure in Riad within a few days. But the beggars were disappointed, for they had hoped that he would turn out to be avaricious, and endeavour to elude them by walking through narrow and lonely streets, where they might catch him. So they pressed more and more upon him every day, trying to exhaust his patience and his charity. In this however they failed, not understanding that the vanity of such a man is inexhaustible and knows no price. Abdullah, too, chose rather to be abroad during the daytime than in the evening or the early morning, for he desired to be seen by the multitude and spoken of as he went through the market-place. Yet on the last evening of all he fell into the hands of the Sheikh of the beggars, and evil befell him.

The hour of prayer was passed and it was almost the time when lights are extinguished. Then Abdullah took his sword under his aba, and also a good knife, which he had proved in battle, and which in his hand would pierce a coat of mail as though it were silk. Almasta, his wife, also made a bundle of woman's clothing and carried it in her arms. For they intended to go to a lonely place by the city wall, that Abdullah might there put on female garments, before entering the palace. He feared, indeed, lest if it were afterwards known by what disguise he had accomplished his purpose, he might receive some name in derision, from which he should never escape so long as he lived. Yet he had no choice but to dress as a woman, since he could not otherwise by any means have gone into the harem.

As he came out of his house, accompanied only by Almasta he was seen at once by the two beggars who were always on the watch. And then, wishing to warn their companions, of whom many were lying asleep upon doorsteps in the same street and in others close by, these two made haste to get up, pretending to be lame and making a great clatter with their staves, as they limped after Abdullah. Then he, who loved to exercise charity in the market-place, but not in the dark where none could applaud him, made a pretence of not seeing the poor men, and went swiftly on with

Almasta running by his side.   But as he walked fast, the two beggars although apparently lame increased their speed with his, and their clatter also.

'Does a sound man need a horse to escape from cripples?' asked Abdullah.   And he turned quickly into a narrow lane.

'It will be wiser to scatter a few coins to them,' said Almasta.   'They will then stop and search for them in the dark.   For these men are very importunate and will certainly hinder us.'

But Abdullah was confident in his legs as a strong man and only walked the faster, so that Almasta could with great difficulty keep beside him.   Then they heard the beggars running after them in the dark and calling upon them.

'O Abdullah!' they cried.   'The light of your charitable countenance goes before us like a lantern, and illuminates the whole street!   Be merciful and give us a small coin, and Allah will reward you!'

Then Abdullah stopped in the darkest part of the narrow lane, seeing that they had recognised him, and conceiving that it would be a reproach for a sheikh of pure blood to run from beggars; and he feared also that it would be remembered against him on the morrow. He therefore made a pretence of being diverted, and laughed.

'Surely,' he said, 'the lame men of Riad could

outrun in a race the sound men of any other city.
And, by Allah, I have little money with me, for I was
going to a friend's house to receive a sum due to me for
certain mares; yet I will give you what I have, and I
pray you, go in peace.'

Thereupon he sought in his wallet for something to
give them, and while he was seeking they began to
praise him after their manner.

'See this Abdullah!' they said. 'He is the father
of the poor and distressed, and is ever ready to divide
all he has with us. Yallah! Bless him exceedingly!
Yallah! Increase his family!'

But when Abdullah had found the money and was
putting it into their hands, he was suddenly aware that
instead of two beggars there were now ten or more, and
these again multiplied in an extraordinary manner, so
that he felt himself hemmed in on every side in a close
press.

'O Allah!' he exclaimed. 'Thou art witness that
unless these small coins are multiplied a hundredfold,
as the basket of dates by the Prophet at the trench
before Medina, I shall have nothing to give these
worthy persons.'

By this time the blind Sheikh of the beggars was
present, and he pushed forward, pretending to rebuke
his companions.

'O you greedy ones!' he cried. 'How often have

I told you not to be so importunate? Yet you crowd upon him like wasps upon a date, presuming upon the goodness of his heart, and when there is no more room you crowd upon each other. Forgive them, O Abdullah!' he said, addressing him directly, 'for they have the appetites of jackals together with the understanding of little children. They would thrust into the dish a hand as small as a crow's foot and withdraw it looking as big as a camel's hoof. Their manners are also——'

'My friend,' said Abdullah, 'I have given what I can. Let me therefore pass on, for my business is of importance, yet the throng is so great that I cannot move a step. To-morrow I will distribute much alms to you all.'

'The radiance of your merciful countenance is enough ·for us,' replied the Sheikh of the beggars, 'and even I who am blind am comforted by its rays as by those of the sun in spring, and my hunger is appeased by the honey of your incomparable eloquence——'

'My friend,' said Abdullah, interrupting him again, 'I pray you to let me go forward now, for I have a very important matter in hand, though it is with difficulty that I tear myself away from your society and I would willingly listen much longer to the words of the wise.'

Then the blind man turned to the other beggars,
and his hearing told him that by this time there were
at least threescore in the street.

'Come, my brothers!' he cried. 'Let us accompany our benefactor to the house of his friend, and
afterwards we will wait for him and see that he
reaches his own dwelling in safety. Surely it is not
fitting that a sheikh of such great consideration
should go about the streets at night without so much
as an attendant carrying a lantern. Let us go with
him.'

Now these last words were the signal agreed upon,
and even as Abdullah began to protest that he desired
no such honourable escort as the beggars offered him,
one came from behind and suddenly drew a thick
barley-sack over his head, so that his voice was heard
no more, and he was dragged down by the throat,
while the one-eyed hunchback caught him by the legs
and bound his feet and four others laid hold of his
hands and tied them firmly behind him. Nor had
Almasta time to utter a single cry before she was
bound hand and foot with her head in a sack, like her
husband. Then at a signal the beggars took up the
two as though they had been bales packed ready for a
camel's back, and carried them away swiftly into the
darkness, towards the eastern gate where the blind
man lived in a ruined house together with three or

four of his most trusted companions. He also sent a messenger to his relation, the Bedouin, as had been agreed. It was already quite dark in the streets and the few persons who met the beggars did not see what they were carrying, nor ask questions of them, merely supposing that they had lingered long in the public square after evening prayers and were now returning in a body to their own quarter.

The blind man's house was built of three rooms and a wall, standing in a square around a small court. But only one of the rooms had a roof of its own, though there was a sort of cellar under the floor of one of the others which served at once as a lodging for beggars in winter, as a storehouse for food when there was any in supply and as a place of deposit for the ancient iron chest in which the common fund of money was kept. To this vault the Sheikh of the beggars made his companions bring the two prisoners, and having set them on the floor, side by side, he proceeded to hold a council, in which the captives themselves had no part, since their heads were tied up in dusty barley-sacks and they could not speak so as to be heard.

'O my brothers!' said the blind man. 'Allah has delivered the enemies of the kingdom into our hand, and it is necessary to decide what we will do with them. Let the oldest and the wisest give their opinions first, and after them the others, even to the youngest, and last of all I will speak, and let us see whether we can agree.'

'Let us kill the man and bury him, and then cast lots among us for the woman,' said one.

'No,' said the next, a man who had twice made the pilgrimage, and was much respected, 'we cannot do this, for the man is a true believer, and evil will befall us if we shed his blood. Let us rather keep him here, and purify his hide every day with our staves, until Khaled is in no more danger, and then we will take him to the palace and deliver him up.'

'It is to be feared,' said the Sheikh of the beggars, 'that the man might chance to die of this sort of purification, though indeed it be very wholesome for him, and I am not altogether against it.'

'Let us make him our slave,' said a third who had himself been the slave of a poor man who had died without heirs. 'The fellow is strong. Let us buy millstones and make him grind barley for us in this cellar. In this way he will not eat our food for nothing.'

After this many others gave advice of the same kind. But while they were talking there was a great clattering and noise upon the stone steps which led down into the cellar, and a man fell over the last step and rolled over and over into the very midst of the council, railing and lamenting.

'It is that ass of Egypt,' said the Sheikh of the beggars. 'I know him by the clattering of the wooden hoofs he wears on his hands, and also by his braying. Let him also give his opinion when he is recovered from his fall.'

'It is strange and marvellous,' said one, 'that he who has no legs should suffer so many falls, being, by the will of Allah, always upon the earth. For when we first saw him we found him fainting upon the ground, having fallen from the wall of a garden, though no man could tell how he had climbed upon it.'

'I had been transported to the top of the wall as in a dream,' replied the cripple, 'for there were dates in that garden. But having eaten too greedily of them I fell asleep on the top and I dreamed that my body was torn by hyænas; and waking suddenly I fell down. For the dates were yet green.'

'This may or may not be true,' said the blind man. 'For you are an Egyptian. Let us, however, hear what you have to advise in the matter of Abdullah and his wife, whom we have taken prisoners.'

'I fear that you mock me, O my lord,' answered the man. 'But if I am mocked, I will advise that this Abdullah be also made a sport of, for us first, and for the people of Riad afterwards.'

'Tell us how this may be done, for a good jest is

better than salt for roasting, and the sheep lie here bound before us.'

'Take this man, then,' said the cripple, 'and uncover his face, and hold him fast. Then let one of us get the razor and shave off all his beard and his eyebrows, and the hair of his head even to the nape of his neck. Then if he came suddenly before her who bore him and cried, "Mother," she would cover her face and answer, "Begone, thou ostrich's egg!" For she would not know him. And to-morrow we will take his excellent clothes from him and put them upon our Sheikh. But we will dress Abdullah in rags such as would not serve to wipe the mud from a slave's shoes in the time of the subsiding waters, and we will tie his hands under his arm-pits and put a halter over his head and lead him about the city. Then he will cry out against us to the people, saying that he is Abdullah, but we will also cry out in answer: "See this madman, who believes himself to be a sheikh of Bedouins though Allah has given him no beard! O people of Riad, you may know that the spring is come, by the braying of this ass."'

'Yet I see now that there may be wisdom in brayings,' said the Sheikh of the beggars, 'though Balaam ibn Beor shut his ears against it, and was punished for his cursing so that his tongue hung down to his breast, all his days, like that of a thirsty dog. This is good counsel, for in this way we shall not shed the man's blood, nor render ourselves guilty of his death; but I think we shall earn a great reward from Khaled, and his kingdom will be saved in laughter.'

During all this time Abdullah had not moved, knowing that he was in the power of many enemies and beyond all reach of help, but when he heard the decision of the Sheikh of the beggars he was filled with shame and rolled himself from side to side upon the floor, as though trying to escape from the bonds that held him. Almasta, for her part, lay quietly where they had put her, for she saw that all chance of success was gone and was pondering how she might take advantage of what happened, to save herself.

Then the beggars laid hold of Abdullah and held him, while others took the sack from his head. He was indeed half smothered with dust, so that at first he could not speak aloud, but coughed and sneezed like a dog that has thrust its nose into a dust-heap to find the bone which is hidden underneath. But presently he recovered his breath and began to rail at them and curse them. To this they paid no attention, but brought the oil lamp near him, and one began to rub soap upon his face and head while another got the razor with which the beggars shaved their heads and began to whet it upon his leathern girdle.

'Do not waste the precious stones of your eloquence

Q

upon a barber,' said the Sheikh of the beggars, 'but reserve your breath and the rich treasures of your speech until you are brought as a plucked bird before the people of Riad. Moreover we only wish to shave off your beard, but if you are restless some of your hide will certainly be removed also, whereby you will be hurt and it will be still harder for your friends to recognise you to-morrow. It is also useless to shout and scream as though you were driving camels, for you are in the cellar of my house which is at a good distance from other habitations, on the borders of the city.'

So Abdullah saw that there was no escape, and that his fate was about his neck, and he sat still as they had placed him, while the one-eyed hunchback shaved off his beard and the hair on his upper lip and his eyebrows, and the lock at the back of his head.

When this was done the blind man put out his hand and felt Abdullah's face.

'Surely,' he said, 'this is not a man's head, but the round end of a walking-staff, rubbed smooth by much use.'

They also tied his hands under his arm-pits and put upon him a ragged shirt with sleeves so that he seemed to have lost both arms at the elbow.

'This is very well done,' said the hunchback turning his head from side to side in order to see all with his one eye. 'But what shall we do with the woman? Let us cast lots for her, and he who wins her shall marry her, and we will hold the feast immediately, for we have not yet supped and there is some of the camel's meat which we received to-day at the palace.'

'O my brothers,' answered the Sheikh of the beggars, 'let us do nothing unlawful in our haste. For this woman is certainly one of Abdullah's wives, as you may see by her clothes, and unless he divorces her none of us can take her for ourselves, seeing that she is the wife of a believer. Take the sack from her head, however, and if she deafens us with her screaming we can put it on again. But you must by no means put her to shame by taking the veil from her face, for she may be an honest wife, though her husband be a dog. If she has done well, we shall find it out, and no harm will have come to her; but if she is a sharer in this fellow's plans, her punishment will be grievous, since she will be the wife of an outcast, having neither beard nor eyebrows and rejected by all men.'

Some of the beggars murmured at this, but most of them praised their Sheikh's wisdom, and would indeed have feared greatly to break the holy law, being chiefly devout men who prayed daily in the mosque and listened to the Khotbah on Friday. They therefore placed Almasta in one corner of the cellar and Abdullah in another, so that the two could not converse together, and then they took out such food as they had and began to eat their supper, laughing and talking over the jest and anticipating the reward which awaited them for saving Khaled.

In the meanwhile the night was advancing and many of Abdullah's friends left their houses secretly and gathered in the neighbourhood of the palace to wait for the first signal from within. By threes and by twos and singly they came out of their dwellings, looking to the right and left to see whether they were not the first, as men do who are not sure of being in the right. All had their swords with them, and some their bows also, and some few carried their spears, and they made no secret of their bearing weapons; but under each man's aba was concealed the largest barley-sack he could find in his house, and concerning this no one of the multitude said anything to his neighbour, for each hoped to get a greater share than the others of the gold and precious stones from the fabulous treasure stored in the palace. Then most of these men sat down to wait, as vultures do before the camel is quite dead. But not long after the middle of the night they were joined by a great throng of Bedouins from Abdullah's tribe. These had been admitted into the city by the watchman according to the agreement, and passed up the great street from the Hasa gate, in a close body, not speaking and making but little noise with their feet as they walked; yet all of them together could be heard from a distance, because they were so many, and the sound was like the night wind among the branches of dry palm trees. After them, other Bedouins came in from camps both near and far, some of them having made half a day's journey since sunset; and they surrounded the palace on all sides, and filled the great street, and the street which passes by the mosque towards the Dereyiyah gate and all the other approaches to the open square, sitting down wherever there was room, or leaning against the closed shops of the bazar, or standing up in a thick crowd when they were too closely pressed to be at ease. They talked together from time to time in low tones, but when their voices rose above a whisper some man in authority hushed them saying that the hour was not yet come.

'By this time Abdullah has slain Khaled,' said some, 'and the daughter of the old Sultan is a prisoner.'

'And by this time,' said others, 'Abdullah is surely unlocking the treasure chamber and filling a barley-sack with pearls and rubies. It is certain that he who slays the lion deserves his bride, but we hope that something will be left for us.'

'Hush!' said the voice of one moving in the darkness. 'Be patient. It is not yet time.'

Then, for a space, a deep silence fell on the speakers and they crouched in their places watching the high black walls of the palace and marking the motion of the stars by the highest point of the tower. Before long whispered words were heard again.

'It would have been more just if Abdullah had opened the gate to us as soon as he had slain Khaled, for then we could have seen what he took. But now, who shall tell us what share of the riches he is hiding away in the more secret vaults?'

'This is true,' answered others. 'And besides, what need have we of Abdullah to help us into the palace? Surely we could have broken down the gates and slain the guards and Khaled himself without Abdullah's help. Yet we, for our part, would not shed the blood of a man who has always dealt very generously with us, nor do we believe the story of the camels laden secretly in Haïl. However, what is ordained will take place, and we shall undoubtedly receive plentiful gold merely for sitting here to watch the stars through the night.'

'The story of the camels is not true,' said a certain man, speaking alone. 'For I was of the drivers sent with them, and being hungry, we opened one of the bales on the way. By Allah! There was nothing but wheat in it, and it was white and good; but there was nothing else, not so much as a few small coins——'

Then there was the sound of a blow, and the man who was speaking was struck on the mouth, so that his speech was interrupted.

'Peace and be silent!' said a voice. 'They who speak lies will receive no share with the rest when the time comes.'

But the man who had been struck was the strongest of all his tribe, though he who had struck him did not know it. And the man caught his assailant by the waist in the dark, and wrestled with him violently, being very angry, and broke his forearm and his collar-bone and several of his ribs, and when he had done with him, he threw him over his shoulder so that he fell fainting and moaning three paces away.

'O you who strike honest men on the mouth in the dark, you have been over-rash!' he cried. 'Go home and hide yourself lest I recognise you and break such bones as you have still whole!'

'This is well done,' said one of the bystanders in a loud voice. 'For the story of the camels laden secretly with treasure is a lie. I also was with the drivers and ate of the wheat. Nor do I believe that Khaled is a robber and a Persian.'

'We do not believe it!' cried a score of Bedouins

together. 'And if we have come here, it is to get our share like other men, since they tell us that Khaled is dead. But now we believe that Abdullah has shut himself into the palace and means to keep all for himself, and is cheating us.'

These men were none of them of Abdullah's tribe, but as the voices grew louder, Abdullah's kinsmen came up, and endeavoured to quiet the growing tumult. The crowd had parted a little and the strong man stood alone in the midst.

'We pray you to be patient,' said Abdullah's men, 'for the time is at hand and the false dawn has already passed, though you have not seen it, so that before long it will be day. Then the gates will be opened and you shall all go in.'

'We have no need of your sheikh to open gates for us,' said the strong man, in a voice that could be heard very far through the crowd. 'And moreover it will be better for you not to strike any more of us, or, by Allah, we will not only break your bones but shed your blood.'

At this there was a sullen cry and men sprang to their feet and laid their hands upon their weapons. But a youth who had come up with Abdullah's kinsmen, though not one of them, bent very low over the man who had been thrown down and then spoke out with a loud and laughing voice.

'Truly they say that crows lead people to the carcases of dogs!' he said. 'This fellow is of the family which murdered my father, upon whom may Allah send peace! Nor will I exceed the bounds of moderation and justice.'

Thereupon the young man drew out his knife and immediately killed his father's enemy as he lay upon the ground, and then he withdrew quickly into the dark crowd so that none knew him. But though there was only the light of the stars and the multitude was great, many had seen the deed and each man stood closer by his neighbour and grasped his weapon to be in readiness. The kinsmen of Abdullah saw that they were separated from their own tribe and drew back, warning the others to keep the peace and be silent, lest they should be cut off from their share of the spoil. But their voices trembled with fears for their own safety, and they were answered by scornful shouts and jeers.

'The young man says well that you are crows,' cried the angry men, 'for you wish to keep the carcase for yourselves. Come and take it if you are able!'

Now indeed the quarrel which had been begun by the blow struck in the dark spread suddenly to great dimensions, for the words spoken were caught up as grains of sand by the wind and blown into all men's ears. Many were ready enough to believe that Abdullah cared only for enriching himself and his tribe, and many more who had been persuaded to the enterprise by the hope of gain turned again to their faith in Khaled as the dream of gold disappeared from their eyes. Yet Abdullah's tribe was numerous, and it was easy to see that if the dissension grew into a strife of arms the fight would be long and fierce on both sides.

Then certain of those who were against Abdullah raised the cry that he had slain Khaled and escaped with the treasure by a secret passage leading under the walls of the city, which passage was spoken of in old tales, though no one knew where to find it. But the multitude believed and pressed forward in a strong body and began to beat against the iron-bound gate of the palace with great stones and pieces of wood. Abdullah's men came on fiercely to prevent them, but were opposed by many, and as the wing of night was lifted and the dawn drank the stars, the wide square was filled with the clashing of arms and the noise of a terrible tumult.

CHAPTER XII

AT the time when the beggars were carrying away Abdullah and his wife, Khaled was sitting in his accustomed place, silent and heavy at heart, and Zehowah played softly to him upon a barbat and sang a sad song in a low voice. For she saw that gloominess had overcome him and she feared to disturb his mood, though she would gladly have made him smile if she had been able.

A black slave of Khaled's whom he had treated with great kindness had secretly told him that there was a plan to enter the palace with evil during that night, for the fellow had spied upon those who knew and had overheard what he now told his master. He had also asked whether he should not warn the guards of the palace, in order that a strict watch should be kept, but Khaled had bidden him be silent.

'Either the guards are conspiring with the rest,' said Khaled, 'and will be the first to attack me, or they are ignorant of the plan; and if so how can they withstand so great a multitude? I will abide by my

own fate, and no man shall lose his life for my sake
unless he desires to do so.'

But he privately put on a coat of mail under his
aba, and when he sat down in the harem to await
the end he would not let Zehowah take his sword, but
laid it upon his feet and sat upright against the wall,
looking towards the door.

'Since I have no soul,' he said to himself, 'this is probably the end of all things.   But there is no reason why I
should not kill as many of these murderers as possible.'

He was gloomy and desponding, however, since he
saw that his hour was at hand, and that Zehowah was
no nearer to loving him than before.   He watched her
fingers as she played upon the instrument, and he
listened to the soft notes of her voice.

'It is a strange thing,' he thought, 'and I believe
that she is not able to love, any more than my sword
upon my feet, which is good and true and beautiful,
and ever ready to my hand, but is itself cold, having
no feeling in it.'

Still Zehowah sang and Khaled heard her song,
listening watchfully for a man's tread upon the
threshold and looking to see a man's face and the
light of steel in the shadow beyond the lamps.

'The night is long,' he said at last, aloud.

'It is not yet midnight,' Zehowah answered.   'But
you are tired.   Will you not go to rest ?'

' I shall rest to-morrow,' said Khaled.   ' To-night I
will sit here and look at you, if you will sing to me.'

Zehowah gazed into his eyes, wondering a little at
his exceeding sadness.   Then she bowed her head and
struck the strings of the instrument to a new measure
more melancholy than the last, and sang an old song
of many verses, with a weeping refrain.

' Are you also heavy at heart to-night?' Khaled
asked, when he had listened to the end.

' It is not easy to kindle a lamp when the rain is
falling heavily,' Zehowah said.   ' Your sadness has
taken hold of me, like the chill of a fever.   I cannot
laugh to-night.'

' And yet you have a good cause, for they say
that to-night the earth is to be delivered of a great
malefactor, a certain Persian, whose name is perhaps
Hassan, a notorious robber.'

Khaled turned away his head, smiling bitterly, for
he desired not to see the satisfaction which would
come into her face.

' This is a poor jest,' she answered in a low voice,
and the barbat rolled from her knees to the carpet
beside her.

' I mean no jesting, for I do not desire to disap-
point you, since you will naturally be glad to be freed
from me.   But I am glad if you are willing to sing
to me, for this night is very long.'

'Do you think that I believe this of you?' asked Zehowah, after some time.

'You believed it yesterday, you believe it to-day, and you will believe it to-morrow when you are free to make choice of some other man—whom you will doubtless love.'

'Yet I know that it is not true,' she said suddenly.

'It is too late,' Khaled answered. 'The more I love you, the more I see how little faith you have in me—and the less faith can I put in you. Will you sing to me again?'

'This is very cruel and bitter.' Zehowah sighed and looked at him.

'Will you sing to me again, Zehowah?' he repeated. 'I like your sad music.'

Then she took up the barbat from the carpet, but though she struck a chord she could not go on and her hand lay idle upon the strings, and her voice was still.

'You are perhaps tired,' said Khaled after some time. 'Then lay aside the instrument and sleep.' He composed himself in his seat, his sword being ready and his eyes towards the door.

But Zehowah shook her head as though awaking from a dream, her fingers ran swiftly over the strings and gentle tones came from her lips. Khaled listened thoughtfully to the song and the words soothed him, but before she had reached the end, she stopped suddenly.

'Why do you not finish it?' he asked.

'If you have told me truth,' she answered, 'this is no time for singing and music. But if not, why should I labour to amuse you, as though I were a slave? I will call one of the women who has a sweet voice and a good memory. She will sing you a kasid which will last till morning.'

'You are wrong,' said Khaled. 'There is no reason in what you say.'

But he reflected upon her nature, while he spoke.

'Surely,' he thought, 'there is nothing in the world so contradictory as a woman. I ask of her a song and she is silent. I bid her rest, supposing her to be weary, and she sings to me. If I tell her that I hate her she will perhaps answer that she loves me. Min Allah! Let us see.'

'You inspire hatred in me,' he said aloud, after a few moments.

At this Zehowah was very much astonished, and she again let the barbat fall from her knees.

'You wished me to believe that you loved me, and this not long since,' she answered.

'It may be so. I did not know you then.'

He looked towards the door as though he would say nothing further. Zehowah sighed, not understand-

ing him yet being wounded in that sensitive tissue of
the heart which divides the outer desert of pride from
the inner garden of love, belonging to neither but
separating the two as a veil. And when there is a
rent in that veil, pride looks on love and scoffs
bitterly, and love looks on pride and weeps tears of
fire.

'I am sorry that you hate me,' she said, but the
words were bitter in her mouth as a draught from a
spring into which the enemy have cast wormwood,
that none may drink of it.

'Allah is great!' thought Khaled. 'This is
already an advantage.'

Then Zehowah took up the barbat and began to
sing a careless song not like any which Khaled had
ever heard. This is the song—

'The fisherman of Oman tied the halter under his arms,
　The sky was as blue as the sea in winter.
　The fisherman dived into the deep waters
　As a ray of light shoots through a sapphire of price.
　The sea was as blue as the sky, for it was winter.
　Among the rocks below the water it was dark and cold
　Though the sky above was as blue as a fine sapphire.
　The fisherman saw a rough shell lying there in the dark
　　　between two crabs,
　"In that shell there must be a large pearl," he said.
　But when he would have taken it the crabs ran together and
　　　fastened upon his hand.
　His heart was bursting in his ribs for lack of breath
　And he thought of the sky above, as blue as the sea in winter.

So he pulled the halter and was taken half-fainting into the
boat.

The crabs held his hand but he struck them off,

And his heart beat merrily as he breathed the wind

Blowing over the sea as blue as the sky in winter.

"There are no pearls in this ocean," he said to his companions,

"But there are crabs if any one cares to dive."

One of them saw the shell caught between the legs of the
crabs,

He opened it and found a pearl of the value of a kingdom.

"The pearl is mine, but you may eat the crabs," he said to
the fisherman.

"Since you say there are no pearls in this ocean,

"Which is as blue as the sky in winter."

Then the fisherman smote him and tried to take the pearl,

But as they strove it fell into the deep water and sank.

Where the sea was as blue as the sky in winter.

"I will drown you with a heavy weight," said the fisherman,
"for you have robbed me of my fortune."

"I have not robbed you, O brother, for the pearl is again where
you found it,

In the sea which is as blue as the sky in winter."

Then the fisherman dived again many times in vain

Till the drums of his ears were broken and his heart was dissolved for lack of breath.

But the pearl is still there, at the bottom of the sea,

And the sea is as blue as the sky in winter.

This is the kasid of the fisherman of Oman

Which Zehowah Bint ul Mahomed el Hamid

Has made and sung for her lord, Khaled the Sultan.

May Allah send him long life and many such hearts

As the one which fell into the ocean

When the sky was as blue as the sea in winter.'

'This is a new song,' said Khaled, when she had finished.

'Is it ? I made it many months ago,' Zehowah answered. 'Does it please you ?'

'It is not very melodious, nor do I think there is much truth in the matter of it. But I thank you, for it has served to pass the time.'

Zehowah laughed a little scornfully.

'I daresay you would prefer the song of a Persian nightingale,' she said. 'Nevertheless my song is full of truth, though you cannot see it. There are many who seek for things of great value and do not know when they have found them because a crab has bitten their hands.'

'Verily,' thought Khaled, 'this is indeed the spirit of contradiction.'

But he was silent for a time, not wishing that she should think him easily moved. In the meantime Zehowah played softly upon the little instrument and Khaled watched her, wondering whether she were not playing upon the strings of his heart, for her own pleasure, as skilfully as her fingers ran upon the chords of the barbat. Many words rose to his lips then, and he wished that he also had the science of music that he might sing sweetly to her. Then he laughed aloud at his own imagination, which was indeed that of a foolish youth.

'The lion roaring for a sweetmeat,' he thought, 'and the sword-hand aching to scratch little tunes upon a lute!'

Zehowah turned suddenly when he laughed, and ceased from playing.

'I am glad that you are merry,' she said. 'I like laughter better than reproaches and prefer it to gloomy forebodings of evil when none is at hand.'

Khaled's face grew dark, and he looked again towards the door.

'If you will stay with me, you shall see that evil is not far off,' he answered, for she had reminded him of what he was expecting, and he knew that it was no jesting matter. 'But you shall please yourself in this as in all other matters, though it were better for you to go now and shut yourself up in an inner room and wait for the end. The night is advancing, and all will soon be over.'

'Hear me, Khaled,' said Zehowah, speaking earnestly. 'If you bid me go, I will go, or if you desire me to stay, I will remain with you. But if you are indeed in danger, as you say, let us call up the guards and the watchmen who sleep in the palace, that they may stand by you with their swords and help you to fight if there is to be strife.'

'I will have no treacherous fellows about me,' Khaled answered, 'and there are none here whom I can trust. My hour is coming and I will fight this fight alone. But if you were such as I once hoped, I would say: "Remain with me, so long as you are safe." Now, since Allah has willed it thus, I say to you: "Go and seek safety where you can find it." Go, therefore, Zehowah, and leave me alone, for I need no one beside me, and you least of all.'

He turned away his head, lest she should see his face, and with his hand made a gesture bidding her to leave him. She rose from her seat softly and hung the barbat upon the wall with the other musical instruments, looking over her shoulder to see whether he would call her back. But he neither moved nor spoke, being resolved to venture all upon this trial, for he knew that if she loved him even but a little, she would not leave him alone in the extremity of danger.

Then she went towards the door of the room, turning her head to look at him as she passed near him.

'Farewell,' she said. But he did not answer nor show that he heard her voice.

As she lifted the curtain to go out, she lingered and gazed at him. He sat motionless upon the carpet, upright against the wall, his sword lying across his feet, his hands hidden under his sleeves, looking towards her indeed but not seeming to see her.

'There can be no real danger,' she thought. 'Could

any man sit thus, expecting death, and refusing to let any one stand by him to fight with him ?   Surely, he is playing with me, and setting a trap for me.   But he shall not catch me.'

She turned to go and the curtain was falling behind her when the night wind from the open passage brought a sound to her ears from a far distance.   She started and listened, as camels do when they hear the first moving of the hot wind.   There were no voices in the noise, which was low and dull, like the breathing of a great multitude and the soft moving of feet, and altogether it was as the slow rising and falling back of the sea upon the shores of Oman, when the great summer storm is coming from the south-west.

Zehowah stood still a moment and drank in every murmur that reached her from without.   Then her face grew white and her lips trembled when she thought of Khaled sitting alone on the other side of the curtain, with his sword upon his feet, waiting for the end.   She lifted the hanging a little and looked at him again.   He saw her, but made no sign.   Even as she looked, the distant murmur grew louder and she fancied that he moved his head as though he heard it.   Then she entered the room and came and stood before him.

'There is a great multitude in the square before the palace,' she said.

'I know it,' he answered, calmly looking up to her face. 'It needed not that you should tell me.'

'Will you not let me stay with you now?' asked Zehowah.

'Why should you stay here?' he asked with a pretence of indifference. 'Of what use are you to me? Take this sword. Can you strike with it? Your wrist is feeble. Or take a bow from the weapons on the wall. Can you draw the string? Your strength is sufficient for the lute, and your skill for scratching the strings of the barbat. Go and save yourself. I am alone and every man's hand is against me.'

Zehowah stood still in the room and hesitated, looking into his eyes for something which she all at once desired with a hot thirst. At last she spoke in an uncertain voice.

'Yet you said not long since that if I were such as you once hoped, you would bid me remain.'

'I do not care,' he answered. 'Yet for your own sake, I advise you to go away.'

'For my own sake!' she repeated, trying to speak scornfully, and turning to go a second time.

But she did not reach the door. She stood still before the weapons which hung upon the wall, and paused a moment and then took a sword from its place. Khaled watched her. She grasped the hilt as

well as she could and swung the weapon in the air
once with all her might.   Then she uttered a little
cry of pain, for she had twisted her wrist.   The
sword fell to the floor.

'He is right,' she said in a low tone, speaking
aloud to herself.   'I am weak and can be of no use
to him.'

. She went on once more towards the door, slowly,
her head bent down, then stopped and then looked
back again.   She feared that she might see a smile on
his face, but his eyes were grave and calm.   Then he
saw her turn and lean against the wall as though she
were suddenly weak.   She hid her face, and there was
silence for a moment, and after that a low sound of
weeping filled the still room.

'Why do you shed tears ?' Khaled asked presently.
'There is no danger for you, I think.   If you will go
and shut yourself in the inner rooms you will be safe.'

She turned fiercely and their eyes met.

'What do I care for myself ?' she cried.   'Among
so many deaths there is surely one for me !'

Even as she spoke Khaled felt a cool breath upon
his forehead, stirring the stillness.   He knew that it
came from the beating of an angel's wings.   All his
body trembled, his head fell forward a little and his
eyes closed.

'This is death,' he thought, 'and my fate has come.

A little longer, and she would have loved me.' But he did not speak aloud.

Again Zehowah's face was turned towards the wall, and still the sound of her weeping filled the air, not subsiding and dying away, but rather increasing with every moment.

'Life is not yet gone,' said Khaled in his heart. 'There is yet hope.' For he no longer felt the cold breath on his forehead, and the trembling had ceased for a moment.

He tried to speak aloud, but his lips could not form words nor his throat utter sounds, and he was amazed at his weakness. A great despair came upon him and his eyes were darkened so that he could not see the lights.

'If only I could speak to her now, she might love me yet!' he thought.

The distant murmur from without was louder now and reached the room, and he heard it. He tried with all his might to raise his hand, to lift his head, to speak a single word.

'It may be that this is the nature of death,' he thought again, 'and I am already dead.'

The noise from the multitude came louder and louder. Zehowah heard it and her breath was caught in her throat. She looked up and saw that the high window of the chamber was no longer quite dark.

The day was dawning.   Then pressing her bosom with her hands she looked again at Khaled.   His head was bent upon his breast and he was so still that she thought he had fallen asleep.   A cry broke from her lips.

'He cares not!' she exclaimed.   'What is it to him, whether I go, or stay?'

Again Khaled felt the cool breeze in the room, fanning his forehead, and once more his limbs trembled. Then he felt that his strength was returning and that he could move.   He raised his head and looked at Zehowah, and just then there was a distant crashing roar, as the Bedouins began to strike upon the gates.

'It is time,' he said, and taking his sword in his hand he rose from his seat.

Zehowah came towards him with outstretched hands, wet cheeks and burning eyes.   She stood before him as though to bar the way, and hinder him from going out.

'What is it to you, whether I go, or stay?' he asked, repeating her own words.

'What is it?   By Allah, it is all my life—I will not let you go!'   And she took hold of his wrists with her weak woman's hands, and tried to thrust him back.

'Go, Zehowah,' he answered, gently pressing her from him   'Go now, and let me meet them alone, knowing that you are safe. For though this be pity which you feel, I know it is nothing more.'

He would have passed by her, but still she held him and kept before him.

'You shall not go!' she cried. 'I will prevent you with my body. Pity, you say? Oh, Khaled! Is pity fierce? Is pity strong? Does pity burn like fire? You shall not go, I say!'

Then her hands grew cold upon his wrists, her cheeks burned and in her eyes there was a deep and gleaming light. All this Khaled felt and saw, while he heard the raging of the multitude without. His sight grew again uncertain. A third time the cool breath blew in his face.

'Yet it cannot be love,' he said uncertainly. Yet she heard him.

'Not love? Khaled, Khaled—my life, my breath, my soul—breath of my life, life of my spirit—oh, Khaled, you have never loved as I love you now!'

Her hands let go his wrists and clasped about his neck, and her face was hidden upon his shoulder while her breath came and went like the gusts of the burning storm in summer.

But as he held her, Khaled looked up and saw that the Angel of Allah was before him, having a smiling countenance and bearing in his hand a bright flame like the crescent moon.

'It is well done, O Khaled,' said the Angel, 'and this is thy reward. Allah sends thee this to be thy own and to live after thy body, saying that thou hast well earned it, for love such as thou hast got now is a rare thing, not common with women and least of all with wives of kings. And now Allah alone knows what thy fate is to be, but thou shalt be judged at the end like other men, according to thy deeds, be they good or evil. And so receive thy soul and do with it as thou wilt.'

The Angel then held out the flame which was like the crescent moon and it immediately took shape and became the brighter image of Khaled himself, endowed with immortality, and the knowledge of its own good and evil. And when Khaled had looked at it fixedly for a moment, being overcome with joy, the vision of himself disappeared, and he was aware that it had entered his own body and taken up its life within him.

'Return thanks to Allah, and go thy way to the end,' said the Angel, who then unfolded his wings and departed to paradise whence he had come.

But Khaled clasped Zehowah tightly in his arms, and looking upwards repeated the first chapter of the Koran and also the one hundred and tenth chapter, which is entitled, Assistance. When he had performed these inward devotions he turned his gaze upon Zehowah and kissed her.

'Praise be to Allah,' he said, 'for this and all
blessings.   But now let us defend ourselves if we can,
my beloved, for I think my enemies are at hand.'

And so he would have stooped to take up his
sword which had fallen upon the floor.   But still
Zehowah held him and would not let him go.

'Not yet, Khaled!' she cried.   'Not yet, soul of
my soul!   The gates are very strong, and will withstand this battering for some time.'

'Would you have him whom you love sit still in
the net until the hunters come to catch him?' he
asked in a tender voice.

'You said you would wait here,' she pleaded.   'If
we must die, let us die here—our life will be a little
longer so.'

'Did I say so?   I thought you did not love me
then, and I would have slain a few only, for my own
sake, that my blood might not be unavenged.   But
now I will slay them all, for your sake, and the
bodies of the dead shall be a rampart for you.'

'Oh, do not go!' she cried again.   'I know a
secret passage from the palace, that leads out by the
wall of the city—come quickly, there is yet time, and
we shall escape—for Allah will protect us.   Surely,
when I was fainting in your arms I heard an angel's
voice—and surely the angel is yet with us, and will
lighten the way as we go.'

'The Angel was indeed here, for he brought me the soul that was promised, if you loved me. And now all is changed, for if we live, we get the victory and if we die we shall inherit paradise.'

And Zehowah looked into his eyes and saw the living soul flaming within, and she believed him.

'If you had always been as you are now, I should have always loved you,' she said softly, and stooping down she took up his sword and drew it out and put it into his hand. 'I tried to wield one when you were not looking,' she said, 'but it hurt my wrist. Come, Khaled—let us go together.'

Then he kissed her once more, and she kissed him, and putting one arm about her, he led her swiftly out by the passage towards the great gate. It was now broad dawn and the light was coming in by the narrow windows.

Zehowah clung to Khaled closely, for the noise of the thundering blows was terrible and deafening, and the multitude without were shouting to each other and calling upon Abdullah to come out, for they supposed him to be in the palace. But the guards and soldiers within had all hidden themselves though they were awake, for there was no one to command them nor to lead them, and they dared not open the gate lest they themselves should be slain in the first rush of the crowd.

Then Khaled and Zehowah paused for a moment near the gate.

'It is better that you should go back, my beloved,' said Khaled. 'Hear what a multitude of angry men are waiting outside.'

'I will not leave you—neither in life nor in death,' she answered.

'Let it be so, then,' said Khaled, 'and I will do my best. For a hundred men could not stop the way before me now, and I think that of five hundred I could slay many.'

So he went up to the gate, and Zehowah stood a little behind him so as to be free of the first sweep of his sword.

'Abdullah!' cried some of the crowd without, while battering at the iron-bound doors. 'Abdullah, thou son of Mohammed and father of lies, come out to us, or we will go to thee!'

'Abdullah, thou thief, thou Persian, thou cheat, come out, and may boiling water be thy portion!'

'Stand back from the gate, and I will open it to you!' cried Khaled in a voice that might have been heard across the Red Desert as far as the shores of the great ocean.

'I, Khaled, will open,' he cried again.

Then there was a great silence and the people fell back a little.

Khaled drew the bolts and unfastened the locks, and opened the gates inward and stood forth alone in the morning light, his sword in his hand and his soul burning in his eyes.

'Khaled!' cried the first who saw him, and the cry was taken up.

The shout was great, and full of joy and shook the earth. For the multitude had grown hot in anger against Abdullah, while they battered at the gates, supposing that he had slain Khaled. But he himself could not at first distinguish whether they were angry or glad.

'If any man wishes to take my life,' he cried, 'let him come and take it.'

And the sword they all knew in battle, began to make a storm of lightning about his head in the morning sun.

Then the strong man who had wrestled and thrown the other before dawn, stood out alone and spoke in a loud voice.

'We will have no Sultan but Khaled!' he cried. 'Give us Abdullah that we may make trappings for our camels from his skin.'

Then Khaled sheathed his sword and came forward from under the gate, and Zehowah stood veiled beside him.

'Where is this Abdullah?' he asked. 'Find him if you can, for I would like to speak with him.'

Then there was silence for a space. But by this time Abdullah's men had fled, for they had already been forced back in the crowding, and so soon as they saw Khaled standing unhurt under the palace gate, they turned quickly and ran for their lives to escape from the city, seeing that all was lost.

'Where is Abdullah?' Khaled asked again.

And a voice from afar off answered, as though heralding the coming of a great personage.

'Behold Abdullah, the Sultan of Nejed!' it cried.

Then the multitude turned angrily, grasping swords and spears and breathing curses. But the murmur broke suddenly into a shout of laughter louder even than the cry for Khaled had been. For a great procession had entered the square and the people made way for it as it advanced towards the palace.

First came a score of lepers, singing in hideous voices and dancing in the early sun, filthy and loathsome to behold. And then came all manner of cripples, laughing and chattering, with coloured rags fastened to their staves, an army of distorted apes.

Then, walking alone and feeling his way with his staff came the Sheikh of the beggars. And in one hand he held the end of a halter, which was fastened about Abdullah's head and neck and between his teeth, so that he could not cry out. And the blind man chanted a kasid which he had composed in the

night in honour of Abdullah ibn Mohammed el Herir,
the victorious Sultan of Nejed.

'Upon whom may Allah send much boiling water,'
sang the Sheikh of the beggars after each stave.

And Abdullah, his head and face shaven as bald as
an ostrich's egg, was bent by the weight he carried, for
upon his shoulders rode the cripple whom they called
the Ass of Egypt, clapping the wooden shoes he used
on his hands, like cymbals to accompany the song of
the blind man. And last of all came a veiled woman,
walking sadly, for she could not escape, being surrounded and driven on by many scores of beggars, all
dancing and shouting and crying out mock praises of
the Sultan Abdullah and his wife.

But as the procession moved on the laughter
increased a hundredfold, until all men's eyes were
blind with mirth, and their breasts were bursting and
aching with so much merriment.

At last the Sheikh of the beggars stood before
Khaled holding the halter. And here he made a deep
obeisance, pulling the halter so that Abdullah nearly
fell to the ground.

'In the name of the beggars,' he said, 'I present
to your high majesty the Sultan of Nejed, Abdullah
ibn Mohammed, and his chief minister the Ass of
Egypt, and moreover the sultan's wife. May it
please your high majesty to reward the beggars with

S

a few small coins and a little barley, for having brought his high majesty, the new sultan, safely to the gate of the palace and to the steps of the throne.'

Thereupon all the beggars, the lepers, the cripples, the blind men and those of weak understanding fell down together at Khaled's feet.

This is the story of Khaled the believing genius, which he caused to be written down in letters of gold by the most accomplished scribe in Nejed, that all men might remember it. But of what afterwards occurred there is nothing told in the scribe's manuscript. It is recounted, however, in the commentaries of one Abd ul Latif that Khaled did not cause Abdullah to be beheaded, nor in any way hurt, save that he was driven out of the city with his wife, where certain Bedouins affirmed that he lived for many years with her in great destitution. But it is well known that after this Zehowah bore Khaled many strong sons, whose children and children's children reigned gloriously for many generations in Nejed. And Khaled and Zehowah died full of years on the same day, and lie buried together in a garden without the Hasa gate, and the pilgrims from Ajman and the east visit their tombs even to the present time.

www.ingramcontent.com/pod-product-compliance
Lightning Source LLC
Chambersburg PA
CBHW031105260626
47172CB00001B/228